ITEM    029 602 882

G000136913

# BESIDE THE SEASIDE

## A COLLECTION OF

## THRILLER, SCIENCE FICTION &

## HORROR

### EDITOR: SCOTT HARRISON

### SNOWBOOKS LTD.

SNOWBOOKS

Proudly published by Snowbooks
Edited by Scott Harrison
With an introduction by David Nobbs

Copyright © 2014 David Nobbs, Sue Wilsea, Gary
McMahon, Trevor Baxendale, J.A. Mains, Sadie Miller,
Alison Littlewood, Lee Harris, Scott Harrison
Front cover image ©National Railway Museum/Science &
Society Picture Library

David Nobbs, Sue Wilsea, Gary McMahon, Trevor
Baxendale, J.A. Mains, Sadie Miller, Alison Littlewood,
Lee Harris and Scott Harrison assert the moral right to be
identified as the author of their work.

All rights reserved.

Snowbooks Ltd
email: info@snowbooks.com
www.snowbooks.com.

British Library Cataloguing in Publication Data.
A catalogue record for this book is available from the
British Library.

Trade paperback ISBN13 978-1-909679-11-5

First published 2014

# Contents

David Nobbs is the author of nineteen novels, including *The Fall & Rise of Reginald Perrin*, *A Bit of a Do*, *Second from Last in the Sack Race*, and his recent bestseller *The Fall & Rise of Gordon Coppinger*. Since his TV writing career began in 1963 he has written sketches and scripts for some of the biggest names in British comedy, such as *The Two Ronnies*, *That Was The Week That Was*, *The Frost Report*, *Frankie Howerd* and *Kenneth Williams*. David has written extensively for BBC Radio4 and penned one-off plays for Granada and Yorkshire Television, as well as providing scripts for a variety of popular sitcoms. Find him at www.davidnobbs.com

# INTRODUCTION

## DAVID NOBBS

A priest friend of mine, working in Nicaragua, was called upon by an uneducated peasant. 'I've heard of things shaped like stones, and you can learn things from them,' said the peasant. He had never actually seen a book, but he wanted to learn to read.

I have to make it clear straightaway that I have a shameful secret. I am not a Yorkshireman. I have only lived in the county since 1992. However, my love affair with the county began long before that, and it began in London, through cricket.

My uncle took me to my first cricket match, Surrey v Yorkshire at the Oval. I was eleven. Looking back, I can recall much of the feel of that day. I can sense the joy in the large crowd that this wonderful game had come to life again after six years of war. It was one of the great days of my life too.

Surrey made not much more than a hundred all out. At the close, Yorkshire were 150 for 5. Hutton, looking as if he was batting on a different pitch from all the others, was 91 not out. He was my hero from that day forth, and still is.

I went to boarding school in 1948, and for five years the only game I could see was the season's curtain raiser at Lords, MCC v Yorkshire. Every year I saw my heroes there, Hutton, Watson, Yardley, Harry Halliday, Bowes...I was Yorkshire through and through, though living, by some strange mistake, in Orpington.

My love of Yorkshire survived ten terrible weeks at Catterick, though even from that period I have a vivid memory of a Sunday off, when I walked up Swaledale and thought I had never seen such beauty in my life. Swaledale imprinted itself on me that day and remains my favourite of the dales.

In 1958, fresh from University, I started my first job, straight back to Yorkshire as a reporter on the *Sheffield Star*. Having my first word in print was a proud moment, and I've never forgotten that first word. It was 'Thives'. 'Thives who broke into the home of Mrs Emily Braithwaite...' Yes, I started with a misprint and it proves a good omen for my success as a journalist.

I wrote for 68 episodes of *Sez Les* with the amazing Les Dawson and two things happened to me which affected my writing career. We were filming in a back street in Leeds, and an elderly lady asked me what was going on. I told her. She was so excited that Yorkshire Television were filming the Les Dawson show in her street. Was there any chance of seeing Les himself? I told her there was if she hung around. She sniffed and said, 'I don't like him'.

Two days later I had cause to complain about the beer in a pub in Hebden Bridge. Not an easy job for a Londoner. 'What's tha got to complain about?' said the landlord. 'Tha never has to come in here again. I've had to drink the bugger for twenty two years.'

I loved this outspoken attitude, and decided to write a novel set in the South Yorkshire I had so enjoyed on the *Star*. Six Yorkshire novels and the TV series *A Bit of a Do* ensued. I met my second wife and have lived in the county ever since.

I have to admit, however, that I am not as familiar with the Yorkshire coast as I would like. There are so many other things to love in this great, proud county – the Dales, the Moors, the exquisite Howardian Hills. Anyway, here goes – an incomer's view of the Yorkshire Coast.

It's a fierce coast, a dangerous coast. There are

beautiful cliff views and walks, but it's a landscape to be treated with caution. Like Yorkshire itself, it's no place for wimps.

But what particularly strikes me is how different in character its towns and resorts are from each other. I'll start at Staithes and work my way South.

Staithes is spectacular. It's like a Northern version of a Cornish village. It has an arty atmosphere, and like most arty places in this rather philistine society, it seemed on my last visit to be struggling. Oh, Staithes, what a difficult path you have to tread between crumbling into decay or reviving into gentility.

It's Whitby that our visitors always want to go to, and it's not surprising. It would be dramatic even without the *Dracula* connection. Whichever way you approach it, along the coast from lovely little Sandsend or over the moors, it's exciting. High above the inner and outer harbour, the gently beautiful church and the forbidding abbey ruins bring a shiver to the spine. I love the tiny old town with its miniscule market and narrow streets, its jewellers selling Whitby jet, its little shops and cafes and all of them independent, and its picturesque alleys. One of them is called Arguments Yard. It could be straight out of *Monty Python*. You can imagine the conversations. 'I agree.' 'Sorry, guv, you can't agree here. This is Arguments Yard.'

The compact village of Runswick Bay, above the attractive bay of the same name, is purpose built for weekenders, their second homes all close together, keeping each other warm. I can see the appeal, but I prefer the charms of Robin Hood's Bay. This narrow, hilly little town is very pretty, but it strikes me as curiously separated from the sea. The sea is there, at the bottom of the hill, but the streets smell of fresh bread and cup cakes and coffee, not of salt.

We are back with the salt and the screams of angry gulls at Scarborough. The county is lucky to have both Whitby and Scarborough. Whitby has the air of a port. Scarborough, though all the ingredients of a port are there, has for me the feel only of a seaside resort. It's undeniably picturesque, with the great sweep of its bay, the castle, the hills and gardens and grand hotels and every kind of entertainment including a great theatre, and I adore the cricket ground. In fact it's one of the great resorts of England, certainly of the East Coast. I'm just not pulled to it as I am to Whitby.

And then we come to Filey. As a comedy writer I have to tell you that Filey is funny. 'Where are you going for your holidays, Ted? Majorca, the Canaries, Barbados?' 'Filey.' This will get a laugh from an audience. No other resort in Yorkshire would get such a laugh. It must just be the name because the place itself isn't funny. The town is compact and quite attractive, the atmosphere is restful, almost sedate, and the beach is superb. This is a place not for day trips and raucous drinking. It's a place for holidays, family holidays, and there aren't many better places in Britain for them.

Between Filey and Bridlington the coast finds a small stretch where it can erupt before succumbing to flatter country. And how it erupts. The great cliffs of Bempton, a paradise for bird watchers such as myself. The amazingly named North Landing. Flamborough Head, the rocks twisted into strange shapes by the merciless attack of the inhospitable North Sea.

And then there is Bridlington. Brid, as we called it in Sheffield. The front starts with a rowdy funfair and subsides into Georgian gentility to the south, and in the middle of it all there is an elegant little old town. There is also a superb entertainment complex. This is the last fling of this dramatic coast, its final statement of its virility.

There's a lot of coast left, down past Hornsea and Withernsea. It is secret and it is lovely, and I don't know it very well. One day, when we don't have visitors who want to go to Whitby, my wife and I will explore it. But it strikes me as one of those places that shouldn't be talked about. You know the kind of articles the press love. 'The last unspoilt village in the Cotswolds', spoiling it for ever.

Hull feels like a city at the end of the world. This is

not a criticism. I like the city very much. It is full of warmth and surprises, and The Land of Green Ginger would be the best street name in the world if it wasn't for Arguments Yard. But Hull's very presence there means that people don't go beyond it very much, and the coast at its bottom end is very little known as it drifts towards the thin spur that is the ever-changing Spurn Head, insecure guardian of the mighty Humber.

These southern parts of the coast, and its immediate interior, are what I think of when I read that Yorkshire masterpiece, *South Riding*, by Winifred Holtby, and published posthumously,which is so sad. This is one of my favourite novels of all time, rivalled by that other great Yorkshire tale, *The Good Companions*, by J.B.Priestley, and an inspiration in my late childhood, *Freedom Farewell*, by Phyllis Bentley, a Yorkshire writer but hardly a Yorkshire classic, being about Julius Caesar.

I have been proud, as a working writer, to live in the county that in my time has produced Keith Waterhouse, Willis Hall and John Braine, and whose literary giants stretch back through Wilkie Collins, Elizabeth Gaskell, and Lewis Carroll, all the way back to Caedmon, the earliest poet of whom any record remains, and who looked after the animals for the monastery of which Whitby Abbey was part.

And that brings me back to the Yorkshire Coast, and

this most welcome anthology. All the stories are set in, and inspired by, places along this coast. The coast and its towns are more than settings. They are integral to the stories; they are characters in the stories.

These stories are about an exciting region. In an increasingly global world the sense of local place is more important than ever. In a world increasingly impressed by gigantism small is not only beautiful but deeply necessary. The short story has become a rather neglected form in recent decades. The great tradition of Yorkshire writing is perhaps not at its most vibrant at the moment. How many good reasons do you need for the publication of this book?

I have dipped into some of the stories, but I have not read any of them. To me, the computer is for writing, not for reading. I will not read these stories on my computer or on a kindle or as an ebook. I will wait, excitedly, until I can read them, as I hope you will, in the proper, dignified setting that they deserve, in a thing shaped like a stone – in that wonderful thing, a book.

Alison Littlewood is a writer of dark fantasy and horror fiction. Her first novel, *A Cold Season*, was published by Jo Fletcher Books in January 2012. Her short stories have appeared in magazines including *Black Static*, *Crimewave* and *Not One Of Us*, as well as the British Fantasy Society *Dark Horizons*. She also contributed to the charity anthology *Never Again* as well as *Read by Dawn Vol 3*, *Midnight Lullabies* and *Festive Fear 2*. Her life writing has appeared in *The Guardian*. Visit her at www.alisonlittlewood.co.uk.

# THAT'S THE WAY TO DO IT

## ALISON LITTLEWOOD

Stevie pulled a face as he jumped off the last step from the promenade, landing in sand that was deep and choppy as a dry bog. He kicked it off his shoes in disgust. The sea seemed a long way down the beach. When he looked up, the castle was a long way off too, its towers jutting dark from the headland which separated him from where he wanted to be.

Scarborough's South Bay was on the other side of the castle; there was noise there, and amusements, and shops. Other kids to play with, maybe. Here there was only his little sister, who squealed with delight as she sank into soft sand up to her ankles.

It was nineteen eighty-five; Stevie was nearly nine

years old, he was on holiday with his mum and dad, and he didn't want to be here at all.

Becky started to squeal and snort and run around in circles, pawing at the air. Stevie sighed. Sometimes he thought it was funny that his sister wanted to be a horse when she grew up; sometimes, he wished she would just turn into one at once and have done with it. She squealed even louder and pointed down the beach. Stevie saw there were donkeys, wearing huge saddles on their backs with metal arches for little kids to hold onto. He sighed again as his mum and dad started to lead the way, without saying a word, towards them.

Mum and Dad watched Becky riding the donkey. It walked up and down, up and down. It was boring; at least, it was until Stevie heard the noise. It was a strange noise, a bit like someone trying to talk through a kazoo. Stevie had got a kazoo in his Christmas cracker that year, but he hadn't thought of trying to talk through it.

He turned and saw a strange sight. There was a tent set up by the sea wall, only it was tiny, just big enough for someone to stand inside. It was painted in red and white stripes, and there was a gap in the front like a serving hatch. In the hatch stood a puppet. It looked like a little red devil, its nose and chin so long they almost touched. It was holding a stuffed baby by one arm, and squealing louder than Becky ever had.

'That's – the way – to do it!' it said, and Stevie only noticed the children sitting cross-legged in the sand when they all started to laugh.

He glanced back over his shoulder; Mum and Dad were still watching the donkey. He wandered casually towards the booth and stood, his arms crossed, behind the other children. Ornate lettering over the tent said *Punch and Judy*. Stevie had heard of Punch and Judy, but he had never seen them. Now a little woman in a white apron came scuttling from the side of the hatch, just as Mr Punch dropped the baby over the side.

The children gasped and then they giggled. Stevie didn't gasp; he frowned. He didn't know why it was supposed to be funny.

Judy screamed and Mr Punch proceeded to hit her with a big stick. The seated children laughed louder.

After a bit there was a crocodile and a policeman, and Mr Punch threw them out of the booth too. Stevie realised his parents were standing behind him. Becky was at his side, fidgeting, but not prancing or galloping or saying a word.

Then the hangman came. He was holding a noose. He waggled it at Mr Punch and told him he had been very, very naughty.

Mr Punch scratched his head. He looked at the

children. 'I don't know what to do,' he said in that high, raspy voice.

So the hangman showed him what to do. He held out the noose and pointed to the hole the rope made. Mr Punch scratched his head again. 'I don't know what to do,' he said.

The hangman showed him again. This time he held out the noose and, pointing, slipped his own head into it; upon which Mr Punch rushed forward and kicked him off the stage. The hangman was hung. He dangled from the booth like an empty bag.

'*That's* the way to do it!' Mr Punch sang out, and the curtains closed and everyone started to get up. They were still laughing. Stevie could hear his mum and dad laughing too. He looked down and Becky wasn't even smiling; Stevie felt a rush of affection for her, but then she looked around at the other kids and up at Mum and Dad and she let out a brief high giggle.

'I don't get it,' he said, but Mum was taking sweet pink sticks of rock from her handbag and so he fell quiet. She gave one to Becky and one to him. He knew Becky would suck hers until it was sticky. He crunched his while they all sat down. He didn't look at Mum and Dad though, or the sea or the castle or anything else. He was watching the back of the Punch and Judy booth, which was bulging and billowing like a ship's sail in a storm.

He got up again and went towards it, just as a large man with purplish cheeks and white whiskers on his chin stepped out. Stevie tried to peer past him into the booth, but the man let the curtains fall closed. He winked at Stevie. 'Trade secrets,' he said. His voice wasn't high and squeaky like before; it was an ordinary voice. He was an ordinary man. He looked a little bit like Stevie's Uncle Bert.

He turned to face Stevie. For a moment his eyes shone back nothing but the flat grey sky, so that Stevie couldn't read his expression. 'What did yer think?' he asked.

Stevie didn't know what to say. Then Becky was there, spinning in circles around him, grinning a pink-stained grin. Her cheeks were pink too while she chanted, 'I love Mister Punch!' and the Punch and Judy man smiled at her. Then he looked once more at Stevie.

Stevie sighed, shaking his sister off. 'I didn't really get it,' he said, and he turned to go, back towards where Mum and Dad were sitting, planning what they'd do later maybe, or what they were going to eat. He didn't look at the Punch and Judy man again. He only heard him as he walked away, letting out a long low sound in the back of his throat. It sounded a little like words, a little like a growl.

* * *

19

They didn't go to the South Bay that afternoon either. They drove past it, Stevie sticking his nose to the car window as they passed shining arcades and a little fairground bright with flashing lights and jangling noise, and then they turned away and headed inland.

'Are we going to Scarborough fair?' Mum said, and Stevie felt a spark of hope until she spluttered and he realised it was supposed to be some sort of joke.

They weren't going to Scarborough fair. Instead they parked on a hill and Dad turned round and said they were going to the park.

'Giddy-up,' said Becky, bouncing up and down in her seat.

So they walked through a little gate and into the greenery and up and around a hill, and Stevie didn't really look at any of it; he was thinking of the fairground, of whooshing up into the air, carried by a Ferris wheel to a land of excitement and adventure. And then there was a lake with an island and what looked like a Japanese pagoda standing on it, and lots and lots of boats, and he drew in a deep breath.

'Are we going on the boats, Dad?'

'Wait and see,' his dad said.

'Neigh,' said Becky.

Mum took Becky's hand and started to tell her a story about the park. It was Peasholm Park, she said, and the pagoda on its island was supposed to look like some sort of plate. A willow pattern, she said, and the picture was all about a love story. There were some people who weren't allowed to be married, but then they got changed into doves and lived happily ever after. Stevie screwed up his nose. He didn't want to know about a plate; plates were boring. He wanted to go on the boats. He pulled on Dad's jacket to ask him again, but then there was a shout and he saw the boats were coming in, all of them; a man was starting to moor them up. Someone else's dad went up to him waving a fiver, and the boatman looked at his watch and shook his head. Stevie sighed.

'Never mind,' said Dad. 'Just wait and see.'

They sat on the banking by the lake. After a while, other people came and sat next to them, and behind them, and in front. It looked as if they were waiting for something to happen. Stevie turned to ask and Dad raised his eyebrows and Stevie fell silent just as a ship sailed into view from behind the rowing boats.

It was a grey ship, a war ship, though it was small; smaller than the other boats. Behind it followed another. And then a man's voice echoed across the lake; it was on a loudspeaker. He told them the names of the ships, and there was a loud crack, and smoke appeared along one of the bows. Becky shuffled in her seat. Stevie sat up straighter. The loud voice told them to jeer at the enemy, and they all went 'boo' as loudly as they could.

There were more loud crashes and bangs; more smoke, and then fire burst from one of the ship's decks. Stevie's face broke into a grin. Becky was still wriggling next to him, but he didn't care. The ships did battle, and he watched, and then there were aeroplanes too, zipping down to drop bombs on the boats, and he could see the wires they flew on but he didn't care about that either. The announcer said something about 'getting a real pasting,' and it made him grin wider. It was great. Much better than the beach; better than anything they'd done so far, even eating sticks of rock or fish and chips.

When it was all over, they walked away. Stevie was still grinning. It had been like something off the telly, only he could still smell the smoke. His mum leaned down and whispered in his ear.

'Really?' he said.

She nodded. 'Actual people inside, steering the ships. Now what do you think of that?'

Stevie imagined being inside one of those ships, bombs dropping about his ears and detonating on the deck just above him, so close he could feel the heat. 'Brilliant,' he said. 'It'd be brilliant, Mum. Being up there doing that, only no one would know it was you.'

Ahead of them, someone stopped in the pathway, as

if they were listening, but Stevie didn't pay any attention to that. He was still thinking about the ships, being *in* the ships, and then they drew near and had to edge around the person on the path, and Stevie looked up and saw it was *him*, the Punch and Judy man, and he was watching Stevie with that same strange light in his eyes.

Stevie swallowed. His throat suddenly seemed dry, as if he had sand in it.

The man leaned down, so that Stevie could smell his slightly stale, slightly sour breath. Each vein on his cheek was visible beneath the reddened skin. He tapped his finger against the side of his nose. Stevie didn't know why.

'Aye, lad,' the man said. Stevie had almost expected his voice to be high and raspy, but it wasn't; it was like he'd heard it before, when he'd walked away across the sand. Low, with a growl in it. 'Aye, you should always appreciate the art, lad.'

Stevie's dad put a hand on his shoulder and started to steer him away, but the man's voice followed them.

'Aye, you should always appreciate what's put on for yer. No matter what it is, eh?'

\* \* \*

That night, Stevie dreamed. He was at the Punch and Judy show, only instead of being in the audience, he was on the stage. It wasn't out in the sun, either; it was lit by a hundred tiny spotlights, shining all around him. The stage was empty. He had something in his hands; he looked down and saw it was a rope.

When he looked up again, someone else was standing on the stage. They were silent and they were watching him. Stevie's mouth went dry. It went dry because he'd forgotten his lines, forgotten what he was supposed to do. He turned the rope in his hands and saw it was a noose.

The man at the other side of the stage was Mr Punch, but this time, he looked different. He had white whiskers on his chin and his cheeks were purple. Even from here Stevie could make out each individual vein threading under the skin.

Mr Punch opened his mouth in a sneer. 'I don't know what to do,' he said, and his voice was mocking. It wasn't Mr Punch's voice, though; it was low and gruff, like the man in the park. It had a growl in it.

And then Stevie knew what he had to do.

He straightened out the rope and he approached Mr Punch. He had to approach Mr Punch because he'd been very, very naughty.

He held out the loop in the noose and gestured towards it. Mr Punch's eyes opened wide and he took a step back. He pointed towards the big blank space in front of the stage. When Stevie looked into that space he could see nothing at all. He heard it, though; sudden bright laughter, loud and meaningless, and yet somehow affirming.

He grinned and held out the noose again. This time, when Mr Punch spoke, he sounded lost: lost and alone and overwhelmingly sad. 'I don't know what to do,' he said.

*It's all right*, Stevie whispered. *It's all right. I'll show you.*

But he found he didn't want to show Mr Punch what to do. He didn't want to do that at all. He didn't know why, not exactly; but he thought, if he did, that something bad would happen. Something bad and final. He wasn't sure how he knew this; only that it was to do with the flat look that had entered Mr Punch's eyes. Their blank shine didn't tell Stevie anything at all, not really, but he knew that was because it was masking something else, something greedy and sly and grasping and *wrong*.

*That's the way to do it*, that hidden thing said.

Stevie started to back away, but Mr Punch was too quick for him. In an instant he darted to the other side of the stage; and he grabbed hold of Stevie, hard, by one of his arms.

*That's the way to do it,* he said, out loud this time, and now it *was* Mr Punch's voice; high and raucous and rasping. *Like talking through a kazoo*, Stevie thought, only it wasn't quite like that, not at all. The laughter was there again too, all around and louder than ever, going on and on so that Stevie thought it would never stop.

He tried to clamp his hands over his ears and found he couldn't. He couldn't do it because Mr Punch still had tight hold of his arm, and because there was something bulky and rough around his neck.

'That's the way to do it,' said Mr Punch, right in Stevie's ear, and the laughter rang out, and Stevie couldn't see anything except that bright light. Then Mr Punch was behind him and the edge of the stage was in front, and Mr Punch's hand was on Stevie's back. He pushed.

Stevie fell. He fell like a rag doll, like an empty bag. He fell for a long time, and there was nothing, nothing but the fall and the laughter and the blank empty shine. Nothing until he felt the air move next to his ear like clammy warm breath, and a little voice said, *jump*.

\* \* \*

Stevie jumped. He didn't know why he jumped, only that he couldn't *not* jump. So he did, feeling himself sinking into something deep, and pushing away with his knees, gaining momentum by waggling his arms. Then he was flying upwards again, up, up, before gravity caught him and he started to fall once more.

He blinked. He couldn't see anything; there was only

light. Somewhere distant and a little distorted, as if heard through layers of water, there was laughter.

*Jump.*

Nothing ahead but the light. But when Stevie jumped, off to the side and a little above him, he could see – something.

*Jump.*

He just wasn't sure what it was.

*Jump. Jump. Jump.*

Stevie's legs were getting tired. His eyes were watering. He couldn't quite see what the thing above him was. Instead he looked out, into the brightness. He forced himself not to blink, and the light started to resolve itself into something.

It was daytime, he knew that; he could tell from the quality of the light, soft and a little greenish, as if filtered through leaves. There were other lights too, and they were shining inward, dazzling him. Spotlights. They were the reason he hadn't been able to see anything, at first.

Now he could. There was a face, peering in at him. There was something wrong with it, and now he focused and saw what it was. The face was too big. It was a little girl's face, but monstrous. Her brown hair was pulled back in pigtails, and she was smiling. Stevie had no idea who she was or why she was grinning like that, straight at him.

*Jump.*

His legs were getting really tired now, but he knew he couldn't stop. If he did he'd sink into the soft thing beneath his feet, and all would be lost. *He* would be lost. He didn't know how he knew that, but somehow he did.

The little girl's expression was changing, her features giant and exaggerated. She pulled a face, then pointed at him. There was another voice, a louder, deeper one, and another face appeared next to hers. It nodded at something away to Stevie's side, and it smiled. It was a man. Stevie could see his eyes, blue and huge, and the thick black hairs sticking out of his nostrils. He grimaced, but the man didn't react. It was as if he wasn't really seeing Stevie at all.

Stevie kept on jumping. He jumped and he twisted his head as far as it would go, and he looked over his shoulder at the thing the man had pointed at. And he saw something he couldn't take in.

There was a big black flea behind him. It swung into view and away; swung into view and away. What surprised Stevie so much, though, besides the flea's unexpected size and its proximity and its *flea*-ness, was that it was riding a brightly painted trapeze.

It swung into view and away. Into view and away.

When Stevie looked around again, the people had gone. *Come back*, he shouted, but no sound came out, only a teeny clicking sound that even he could hardly hear. *Come back.*

Now there were no people, not even his mum and dad; not even Becky.

*Help.*

He should be waking up now, he told himself. Any moment, he would; it would be all right. He'd get up and eat cereal in the little breakfast room at the B&B, and he wouldn't complain. He'd even smile when Becky asked if she could eat out of a nosebag like horses did.

*Jump.*

He looked down and saw the thing his feet kept sinking into. It was wide and white, and at first he couldn't tell what it was; then he had it. It was a trampoline. An ordinary trampoline. His legs, though, didn't look right; they didn't look right at all. They were too thin for one thing, and they were too black and too hairy. His knees bent the wrong way. They weren't the legs of a nine year old boy who was on holiday with his mum and dad and his little sister.

He looked outward again so that he wouldn't have to look at his legs any more. He didn't want to see them, didn't want to think about them. And he realised that, close to his eyes and a little above him, something was written backwards on the air. No, not on the air, on glass. On the other side of the glass screen in front of him. He made out the letters one by one. *Flea Circus*, it said, in bright cheerful letters.

*God*, he thought. *Oh, God.*

He had seen it before, he knew. He'd seen it on their walk through Peasholm Park. He'd looked at it, but hadn't really paid attention. He hadn't *seen*.

Stevie kept on jumping. It was what he had to do; it was all he could do. He kept on jumping and he kept on not waking up. After a while, more faces came and looked at him. They looked and he screamed for help and the clicking sound came out, and they laughed and then they went away. *Come back*, he thought.

But they didn't.

\* \* \*

The fleas danced. The fleas spun and they swung through the air and one flea, just one, jumped up and down for all it was worth. *Stevie*, it thought. It kept reminding itself its name was Stevie.

Sometimes the thought was clearer than others. Sometimes he drifted, always moving but without thinking, just forcing his aching legs to move until it felt like something mechanical. Sometimes, he called out to the others. They were all around him but not with him, not really. They didn't seem to want to talk. Once he got a rasping chitter from the trapeze artist as it flew above him, and he thought there was a voice in it, but it was a dull voice. Dull and mechanical, as if its thoughts were dull and mechanical too, and terror rose in Stevie as he heard it and he wondered if, one day, his thoughts would be like that as well.

From time to time the view changed as people looked in. They were mostly children, and some of them laughed; some of them sneered. Some just looked bored, or tired, or bewildered. And then Stevie's legs hurt more than ever, jumping up and down so hard, trying to make them *see*.

At those times, he thought of his mum and dad. The way it had been, that last day; watching the ships cutting through the water, the spurts of smoke and flame. The way he had grinned, the feel of it on his face, that bright expression. He hadn't seemed to be able to stop grinning.

*Brilliant*, he'd said. *It'd be brilliant, Mum. Being up there doing that, only no one would know it was you.*

And then the memory of that grin would fade, and there was only the glass, and the laughter, and the people who didn't seem to really look at him at all.

Then there was the day his mum and dad came.

His dad looked older. His face was more lined. Mum looked older too; there were grey streaks in her hair. Becky was with them, and she was taller than she had been before. She didn't run around and she didn't prance.

*Good*, thought Stevie, although he couldn't really have said why.

They didn't look sad. He couldn't tell if they missed him. He jumped high for them, higher than he had ever jumped before, and his sister laughed; he could hear it through the glass, a bubbling trill that was like water and went on and on. And then Stevie's heart felt lighter too and he flew through the air, and when he saw her smile it seemed his legs didn't hurt at all.

After that, it seemed better. He would make the children smile, he thought, and it would be all right; if he could only make them smile. And as he jumped, words drifted through his mind: words he thought he might have heard, once. *You should always appreciate the art, son*, that voice said. And Stevie did. Yes, he thought, as he jumped up and down on the trampoline, over and over, trying to make the children smile; he *did*.

And then the children stepped aside and he saw the Punch and Judy man.

His whiskers were longer than they had been before, and his cheeks more purple. His nose was purple too, and rounder than Stevie remembered; but it was definitely him. He could tell by the flat shine in his eyes, like dull grey clouds that went on forever.

The Punch and Judy man leaned in and his lips twisted into a half-smile, half-sneer. His breath misted the glass and he wiped at it with a grimy coat sleeve.

Stevie wanted to run away, but of course he didn't. He just kept on jumping; he couldn't do anything else.

The Punch and Judy man looked at Stevie as if he knew exactly who he was. Then he nodded, as if he knew what Stevie was thinking.

He leaned in closer and mouthed something through the glass. Stevie looked back at him. He couldn't hear the words, but he knew what the Punch and Judy man had said, and he knew the way his voice would have sounded, if he'd heard it: high and raspy like someone speaking through a kazoo, and he couldn't stop the man from looking and he couldn't stop jumping even though his legs hurt and he felt suddenly tired, so tired, and he didn't know why he was doing it any longer but he couldn't seem to stop: jump, jump, jump.

The Punch and Judy man smiled. *That's the way to do it*, he said.

Lee Harris is the Senior Editor at Angry Robot Books; he is also the former publisher of *Hub* (a monthly short fiction dead tree zine, which became a weekly online publication before half-collapsing at issue 150). He also writes — mainly short stories, though he has written for the stage, too, and he's partway through writing a novel — but then, isn't everyone? He's married with two beautiful young daughters, and has far too many unread books and unwatched DVDs — not that that would ever prevent him from buying more! He hates dried fruit, but loves mince pies, and no — he doesn't understand that, either.

# LANDLADY INTERFACE

## LEE HARRIS

As soon as I stepped over the threshold of Primrose Cottage, I knew it was the guest house for me. I've always liked traditional, and Primrose was as trad as they came. Old-fashioned, even. It was the first time I'd been allowed through the coastal wall into what used to be known as Robin Hood's Bay – the last time my permission had been verified I'd been sick, and it was too late to transfer the date. Data might be insta, but beaurocracy – as ever – ruled the networks. I was looking forward to experiencing some custom landlady interware first-hand, and this was definitely the place in which to do it.

The house AI was running an older version of the Gibson suite – sixteen, perhaps seventeen updates out of sync – and the floor runnerlites were a dead giveaway. The AI might be rudimentary, but it was positively state of the art when compared with the localised hardware. The runnerlites even appeared to be *bulbed*, for Chrissakes, and the least said about the wavecatchas, the better (all optical, it appeared)!

Like all Gibsons, the AI was partially voice-, partially gesture-driven. It was difficult to tell whether the owners had installed as early adopters and never upgraded, or if they'd deliberately retrograded to attract the nostalgians. In any case, it would take at least thirty minutes for the system to recognise me by gait, so until then I'd have to vocally interface. I'd netbooked, so my voiceprint would already be on file. Theoretically.

The system waited for me to direct it. Newer clients of course would autopredict my needs based on historically-similar bookings I'd made across the grid – at least that's what the site-copy said. As every LLI I'd ever interacted with had simply directed me – holo-optically, or otherwise – to my guest suite as soon as I arrived, I suspected it was a work in progress. This particular Gibson just waited until I instructed it. A, it might be – I it most certainly was not!

Rather than vocommand, I gestured my hand forward, palm up, to see if the LLI would interpret correctly. It did.

"Your room is this way. Please follow me." The voice

was friendly, and humanseem. It didn't have the omni-sound quality of the latest models, but appeared to be coming from *actual hardwired speakers!* Not only that, but the runnerlites started juicing, and I was able to follow them across the walls and up the stairs – *stairs!* – to my suite. I swear, if my grin had been any wider at this point I'd have damaged some facial muscles! The door opened as I approached, even though it was far too soon for gaitrec to be up to speed – the system was just dumb enough to assume the person following the runnerlites was the guest, and just smart enough to follow the guest from ingress to ingress to prevent accidental misrec.

Perfect.

I'd booked a See View room – one with an actual window (so quaint!) instead of a scapescreen, and one which faced the main entrance to the guest house, so I could observe the comings and goings of everyone into and out of the place. I waited outside my door for a moment to see if the AI would prompt me, but it waited until I was insuite before replaying a standard welcome message and instructional voc. The system would eventually rec my gait, of course. Until then it would operate almost exclusively on vocommands, though some standardised gestures would be accepted and it might attempt to interpret any personal ones I cared to use, tying them to prompted vocommands if unsuccessful.

Oh, this was going to be fun! And profitable, too, I hoped.

"What is your designation?" I asked the LLI.

"Call me Ivy," came the reply.

"Well, Ivy," I said, "you and I are going dancing!"

\* \* \*

Ivy proved to be a surprisingly competent dancer, and I had to break out some unexpectedly complex moves to get her to show me what she had hidden behind the wheezy voice that came from my suite's speakers, but show me she did. After only a few short hours I'd successfully managed to reverse engineer the gait of every guest currently staying at Primrose, though I had never met any of them, and had no way yet of matching the gait with the gaitee. When Ivy had been programmed, way back in the day, gait recognition was the next big thing – identifying people by the way they move, rather than the way they look was something an AI was particularly suited to, but no-one had expected anyone to deliberately mimic the way others moved; it was believed impossible to do successfully, so few security measures were introduced, at first. Different these days, of course. But everyone has a talent – and movement happens to be mine. That, and a keen interest in computational history. I was now able to successfully mimic everyone in the building, and that meant I could access their rooms without anyone knowing I'd been there. And if the police were called? Well, the LLI records would show that the correct guests had entered their own rooms, so as far as the authorities are concerned, there would be no crime.

You gotta love oldtech.

* * *

My first attempt at using gaitrec to enter another guest's room was only partially successful. I watched through my window until I saw the first guest leave. I only saw him from behind, but I didn't need to know who he was – I just needed to recognise the way he moved, and recognise it, I did – I'd been practising it for long enough, that day. Once he'd turned the corner at the end of the street, I headed downstairs (*stairs! Still grinning!*) and left the building as myself. The LLI now knew we were both outside. I walked down the road, waited for a few minutes and then walked back, mimicking the absent guest's walk. The door opened as I approached, and I gestured for the LLI to direct me to my – his – room. The runnerlites came on, and I was directed to my first victim's square. The door opened on my approach – it worked! – and I was about to enter when a voice came from inside the room.

"Jonas, is that you?"

He wasn't staying alone! The mimicking had worked, but I hadn't taken into account the existence of additional guests within the same squares! I gestured for the door to close, and headed back to the entrance, only just remembering to use *his* moves instead of my own – it had been easy enough to fool Ivy, but I didn't want to test her dupe error routines, when – or if – she noticed that a guest she had registered as exiting the property was somehow back inside! I left and walked a hundred steps or so – probably overkill, but I wanted to be sure I was out of the house's scan-range.

A few minutes later I walked back up to the house as me, and went to my square to sit down. This was going to take a little bit more effort than I'd anticipated!

It was becoming obvious that I needed to get to know who was in the cottage with me – who was on their own, and who had come with company. But how to do it without looking suspicious? I couldn't simply knock on people's doors – when the crimes were reported, that would be the first thing that everyone would remember!

Gazing out of my See View (I don't think I'd ever get used to having an actual *window* in my room!) I noticed another guest, leaving, and an idea struck me. I resolved to follow him and see where his travels took him.

I picked up my jacket, which I'd flung onto the bed, as the weather outside looked to be taking a turn for the worse, and I headed downstairs. As I entered the hallway, a woman came out of another doorway too rapidly, and our shoulders collided.

"I'm so sorry," I said. "Are you OK?"

"It's fine," she replied, smiling. "It was my fault, anyway. I should have been looking where I was going. I'm still getting used to the LLI, and I think I was gesturing a little to flamboyantly, and not concentrating on what was in front of me."

She was cute. That was the first thing I noticed about her. She was also about my age, which didn't hurt. I noticed the jet bracelet on her left arm, though. I gestured toward it.

"Is that real?" I asked.

"What?" She looked confused for a moment. "Oh, the bracelet. Yes. I'm not sure I should be still wearing it, actually..." Now it was *my* turn to look confused. "Long story," she said.

"Well, I have time," I replied. "Perhaps you could tell me over a drink?" I paused, weighing up the situation. "I'm sorry – that was too forward of me. You don't know anything about me, and you're obviously in a hurry." I rubbed my shoulder to emphasise the point.

She laughed and thumped me in the shoulder – deliberately, this time.

"Ow!" I said, with some conviction.

"Well, now I really *do* have to apologise," she said. "The first drink is on me. I don't know anyone around here, and it would be nice to have someone to talk to. I have to warn you, though – I might not be the best company, tonight."

We wandered for maybe half a K until we chanced upon a bar that didn't look too run-down, and we went in. It didn't look as old-fashioned as the guest house, but it *did* have more than one person behind the bar – an unusual sight, these days. Either the owners used bar staff deliberately, else the dispensers had broken down. Neither explanation would have particularly surprised me, given the state of the place. My companion – she'd introduced herself as Kit on the walk here – pointed at them in wonder.

"Do you think they don't realise how inexpensive dispensers are? Why use real staff? One, I can understand, but three?"

"I know," I said. "But I quite like it. It reminds me of some of the books I read in U. I think it adds a touch of authenticity, don't you?"

"Yes, but authentic *what*?" asked Kit.

"What can I get you?"

"Oh no," she said. "It's on me, remember? I'm the one who caused the bodily grievance – the least I can do is buy you a drink."

I sat down and said, "Well, whatever their local brew is, then, thanks."

She walked to the bar and I heard her give the order. Fascinatedly, she watched the bar person as he fulfilled her order, by pouring drinks directly from a clay jug – just like they did in the late twentieth. More fascinatedly, I watched *her*. She was my age, or thereabouts, but she didn't seem it. She moved and gestured like... well, not like a child, exactly, but with child-like enthusiasm. I couldn't quite put her finger on it – it was almost like she hadn't had the optimism beaten out of her like most people I knew. It was tough all round, but Kit looked like she was not only coping, but *enjoying* life. I knew there was a story there – the jet bracelet was part of it, certainly – and I found myself looking forward to hearing what it was. Thoughts of my on-going duplicity temporarily expunged from my mind.

"Here. Drink this," she said, placing before me a drink that looked... Well, it didn't look like the sort of thing you should put *near* a person, never mind *in* one!

"What the–"

"I'm told it's fine," she said, staring at the murky brown, gloopy liquid with as much mistrust as I. "The bar server person said it's a local delicacy. Made from... well, you probably don't want to know what it's made from, but he assures me it's good."

I sniffed at my glass and decided I'd be in for a credit. I lifted the glass to my lips and –

"He said just to make sure you sip it slowly, not all at–"

Too late. The entire contents of the glass was in my mouth, and I couldn't help but swallow half of it. It burned as it went down, but behind the pain I was dimly aware of a rather pleasant flavour. A bit fishy, perhaps, but sweet, and a little unusual. I spat the rest of the drink back into the glass, and looked up to see Kit's horrified face, and behind her, the amused grins – and in one case, outright laughter – of the bar servers.

I wiped my mouth. "I'm all right," I said, waving to the room, generally, though no-one else had taken any notice. "I could do with a water, though," I called to the bar. Still grinning, one of them filled a glass and brought it over.

"You really should just sip that, you know," he said.

"You think?"

Kit's hand shot to cover her mouth, and she stifled a giggle.

"I blame you for this, you know. Let's see you try yours, then." I indicated her glass.

To my surprise, she drank it in one, and seeing the shocked expression on my face, said, "Choc smoothie."

The rest of the evening went well, and we walked back to Primrose Cottage together. Despite her initial warning, she was very good company indeed, and it was with a tinge of regret that I left her at the door to her square and headed up the stairs to mine. I needed to get some sleep – I had a busy day planned.

\* \* \*

I woke early when I heard the satisfying *clang* of the front door closing. The dampeners were evidently off, but I liked the fact that not everything in the place worked as well as it should – for one thing, it meant I got a heads-up when someone was leaving.

Again, I recognised the tenant from his gait, and I pulled the old leaving-as-me/returning-as-him routine. The adventures of the previous evening meant I hadn't had the opportunity to research the rest of the guests, as I'd meant to, so before entering the square this time I stood in the doorway and peered in, satisfying myself that the area was free. I entered, being careful to mimic the guest's actions all the while, and looked around. There was a cell on the desk – no use. Highly traceable. There was also a high-end viewscreen. Also traceable, but the tech was easier to hack. That would fetch a couple of weeks' salary, at least! I switched it on and turned off the sofTrack suite. That would have to suffice until I was in my own space and could permanise it. I stuffed it in the bag I had brought for the purpose, and continued to look around. A few credbills and some paper docs – nothing worth bothering with. Oh, well – the VS was good enough to have made the effort worthwhile.

I left the way I came, and headed down the road a while. After turning the corner I changed my gait back to my default and headed back to my square.

I was able to hit four more guests by the end of the day, and while my haul wouldn't make me rich, it more than paid for my trip and besides – it was fun! I found a dark blue homberg in the third room, and that alone made the whole thing worthwhile! Old school!

Just as I was thinking it was time to head out for some dinner, I heard a knock on my door. I gestured for the door to open, and Ivy obliged. Kit was standing there, holding a bottle of something that looked temptingly alcoholic.

"There's a great BYOB on the seafront," she said. "Fancy coming?"

I smiled, grabbed my coat, and we headed out.

We polished off Kit's bottle with ease. The food was good, and Kit insisted on popping out to grab another bottle for us to consume. She was gone less than fifteen minute – blaming the slow nature of seaside taxi services for even that short delay –  and we finished the second bottle just as easily.

We headed back to Primrose and she pulled me into her square.

She kicked me out again three hours later, and I staggered back to my room, happy, content, and extremely tired.

When I woke the next morning, it took me a while to work out that something was amiss. I checked under my bed, and discovered nothing. Which was a problem, as that was where I'd stashed all of the items I'd pilfered the previous day.

What to do? What to do?

Someone evidently knew my secret, and had stolen my ill-gotten gains away from me. The cheek of it! And the worst thing was, I couldn't report it to Ivy or the authorities. I checked the rest of my room – all my own goods were present and correct. Whoever had broken in had taken the trouble to only steal the stolen items. Very clever! I would have been impressed, if I wasn't so annoyed.

Well, there was little I could do right away, and the

vague alcoholic fug of the previous evening made me hungry. I walked down to the lounge for breakfast, and saw Kit sitting alone.

"May I join you?" I asked.

"Yes, of course. Do."

She smiled, but it was an uncomfortable smile.

"Something wrong?" I asked.

She paused before answering. "I have to go home. I really enjoyed your company last night, and I wish I could have stayed a bit longer but I've been called back. It's complicated. Can I give you my edress and I'll explain later?"

I nodded, and she handed me a card emblazoned with her name, her cell and her edress.

I was about to say something – I wasn't sure what – when I was cut off by Ivy.

"Cab waiting for Kit Smithson. Cab waiting for Kit Smithson."

I made to stand, but Kit shook her head. "Just write," she said.

Her cases had already been packed and they stood inside the door; Kit pulled them along and a moment later I heard the door open and slam. I wandered to the window and saw the cab driver help Kit load her cases into the back, before they both entered the cabin.

Kit turned, and saw me watching through the window. She smiled.

Then she *smiled*.

She reached into her bag and brought something out. It was too dark for me to see it clearly, at first, but when she put it on her head I recognised it at once. A blue homberg. She laughed and waved, and I knew I would never see her again.

I looked down at the card she'd given me. Her cell and edress were no longer there – If they ever *were* her real contact details, which I doubted. In their place were the words "Thanks for the gifts."

And let's face it – the souvenirs are always the best part of a seaside outing, aren't they?

Sadie Miller's short stories have been published by Gothic City Press, Prole Magazine and Oddville Press, with forthcoming work appearing in Static Movement's *Shape Shifters Anthology* and *Black Heart Magazine*. She is a regular writer and contributor for *Excessica* books, with two novellas available to download and a novel in the works. Her poetry has been published by the *Red Booth Review, Clockwise Cat* and *The Commonline Journal*, and her audio play is currently in development with Audio Scribble for a Christmas 2014 release.

# SCARBOROUGH IN JULY

## SADIE MILLER

There are places in the world where the sun touches it once or twice a year, and on those days everything becomes illuminated. The past and the present come together in a glinting spectacle, and grey days are forgotten, as if they had never really happened at all. Today was one such day.

A girl with long black hair woke up in her bedroom on the outskirts of town, the sun streaming through the gap in the curtains, warming the room up for the day. The trees outside cast shadows against the curtains as the dappled sunlight shone through. The girl turned over in her bed, the sun already hot against her face. Her hair had dried in odd clumps against her pillow, wet from her nighttime swim.

She could hear her younger sisters downstairs squealing in high spirits, excited for the prospect of a few glorious weeks of freedom from school that stretched out ahead of them, just waiting to be filled with adventures. There was the sound of cereal hitting bowls, the fridge opening and slamming shut a few times, and loud strains from the television, which was always on in the background.

She swung her legs out of bed, tied back her hair into a messy ponytail, and so her day began.

*   *   *   *

In the Grand Hotel, the actress sat up in bed, a cup of tea cooling on the bedside table. Her well-thumbed script sat creased beside her on the covers, and through the open curtains she could see the blue of the sky and the white of the sands, which stretched out long and flat, punctuation by the red houses behind. The sea was as turquoise as any in the south of France, or Mediterranean, she thought as she pushed the red hair away from her face, and brushed down the peach coloured bedcovers. Outside, seagulls weaved their dance through the sky, their cries honking and joyful.

The actress gave a loud sigh. A difficult inner debate was raging. Should she take breakfast in her very agreeable bedroom, or the terrace? There had already been a couple in the lobby who had recognised her. She remembered checking in her cases, vaguely seeing them staring at her from their place on the sofas.

"Excuse me, I hope you don't mind me asking, but my husband and I are sure we recognise you from somewhere! I don't suppose you are – an actress?" the woman had said, edging towards her slowly until they were side by side at the front desk. The actress had taken her room key from the young man behind the desk, and shook her head at them.

"No, so sorry. You must be mistaking me for someone else."

The woman had looked crestfallen, and returned to her husband shaking her head and mouthing an exaggerated 'No'. The actress had smiled secretly to herself, and made her way up to her room.

The Grand Hotel faced right out onto the sea front, and the actress breathed in deeply. Much better than dirty London air, she thought. There was already an invitingly salty smell from the seafront below, and she gave a little chuckle to herself.

*　*　*　*

Outside her small house, the girl with the black hair
pulled the door shut with difficulty, as it had swollen
with the summer weather. Her little sisters were at the
window, their noses pressed flat and white against the
glass. She waved goodbye to them, and then the girl
tucked her long black hair behind her ears as she walked
down the path and off through the town centre.

She headed down Cliff Street, which had become
rougher around the edges in recent years. The Stephen
Joseph Theatre punctuated the end of the street leading
down into the main area of shops, a favourite with locals
and tourists alike.

Scarborough was unremarkable, the girl thought,
walking past a bench where the local tramp lay swathed
in everything he owned, grunting to himself between
his fitful dreams. A small dog slept inconspicuously
underneath the bench, shading himself. The sun was
indeed high this morning, and the girl made her way
along the pavements, careful to avoid the scatterings of
chewing gum and seagull droppings, her long pale legs
gleaming.

A large man walked past her, already damp with
sweat, a thick film of moisture settling across his face.
He struggled to carry his newly purchased flat screen

television, and two small children raced around his legs, pulling at his t-shirt as they hid from one another around his large belly, threatening to bring him and the television toppling to the ground.

"Stop that now, come back here!" he shouted at them breathlessly and the pair tore off down the high street.

Groups of young girls were milling around, all dressed in shorts and cropped t-shirts, hair swinging down their backs. The girl with the black hair imagined they were going down to the old theme park, which was abandoned now. It had become the best place for girls and boys her age to go and pretend they were alone in the world.

She made her way to the fish and chip shop where she had worked since she was eleven years old, as young as her sisters, and had never thought about leaving. The sign above had some paint peeling off, even though it was a new sign, only a few years old. A bell rung as she pushed through the door, and her friend gave her a sleepy morning wave from behind the counter.

"Morning," the girl with the long back hair replied softly.

They weren't officially open yet, but already there was a potent smell of fish and fat, which somehow wasn't unpleasant. She went behind the bubbling counter into the back room to put down her things and begin the first jobs of the day.

The back office was cool and smelt of disinfectant. She tucked her long black hair into her hair net. It was going to be an intensely hot July day outside, one of those days that comes out of nowhere and burns all it's heat out in a single afternoon. The air conditioning unit buffered the magazines on the racks, and the table menus fluttered against the strong gusts.

High season was in full swing, and tourists were beginning to wander past. Some peered in with interest, making a mental note to walk back that same way after a day at the beach. Some rushed in already, keen to order even though they had only finished a large hotel breakfast minutes before. She smiled at them. They had come from other places, to visit and enjoy the quaint bustling magic of the town. She lived there, as her family had always done. The photos on the mantelpiece at home, the little boats and her grandmother in a big skirt on the beach. The Spa and the Japanese gardens. The Albanio. The fish fizzled violently in their sea of hot oil, and hissed as they came up in batter and funneled into paper containers, golden and inviting.

\*   \*   \*   \*

Anne was a local woman, a few years older than the girl with the black hair, but somehow she seemed so much older. The day had begun for most people, but she was still home, waiting anxiously for the postman. If he hasn't come by 9.30am, she would have to leave anyway, she decided. Her bag for the day was already packed with everything she would need. Her favourite hat, her favourite book and an umbrella, just in case. She opened her purse again to count her coins, and check she had enough for her morning treat. She looked outside again, but the street was empty. A few cars drove past, some very fast and some slow and cautious, it was after all a steep hill. Her mother didn't like her to go out before the postman came, just in case it was something important. Her mother would be asleep upstairs now until well past midday, her sickly breaths coming in fits and starts. If the postman came whilst she was out, her mother would never hear him and then she would be furious at Anne. She would turn and look out of the window and cough dramatically, and Anne would slink back downstairs into the dark of the living room.

On mornings like these, she really missed her father. She had remembered him taking her to the Japanese gardens when she was a little girl, how she had sat next to him as he read the newspaper, and had listened as he murmured the words aloud.

Her book was heavy in her handbag, waiting to be read, and she was keen to leave. She peered out of the curtain one more time. Next door's cat jaunted past, glancing up at her imperiously.

"Shoo!" the woman made a gesture with the net curtains. The cat ignored her, and settled onto the brick garden wall, which the sun had made warm. The woman glanced at the clock one more time, made her decision, and headed out into the sunshine.

The boy relaxed his shoulders under the warmth of the sun on his back. He hadn't live in Scarborough very long, but already the boy felt he knew the town and could quite comfortable pass for a local. He was small but stocky, with the slim neat features that were part of his Eastern European heritage. His hair was usually an unremarkable shade of brown, but life in this surprisingly sunny town had given it a golden hue. He turned the corner and could see the sea stretching out invitingly in the distance. The hotel where he worked was perched on the edge majestically; Queen of all she surveyed. He coughed anxiously to himself, pulled at his shirtsleeves, and walked through the door of the fish and chip shop.

Anne the local woman followed in close behind him, bumping past him with her large handbag. She had run part of the way and now she was here she looked anxiously around her, then gave an inner sigh of relief as she saw that her favourite table was still unoccupied. It was right by the window, and gave her a good view of everyone outside whilst she had her first tea and cake of the day. There was already a long queue, so she settled herself at the table, and waited patiently in the cooling breeze of the air conditioning.

The girl with long black hair was wiping down the Formica tables. The boy hadn't planned to eat in, but she had seen him staring at her, and so he sat down at the table, nonchalantly, as if this had been his intention all along. The girl walked across to him to take his order.

"Good morning," he said, without any idea what he was going to say next.

"Morning. What would you like?"

"A tea please – no, coffee, – and one of those bun things, to take away."

She smiled at him again,

He tugged at the collar of his shirt, which was rubbing slightly at the razor rash on his neck. Nervously, he pulled out an envelope from his pocket, and laid it on the table. The girl walked back towards him, black tendrils of hair wriggling free from her hair net. She carried a small cup of coffee and a little polystyrene box, which was already a little greasy from the bun inside.

"Here you go," she said softly, and smiled again "There's sugar on the table behind you,"

"Oh yes, yes, thank you," he started to say, but she had already walked away again. The tickets sat on the table, looking at him expectantly. There are two of us, they said. Why don't you ask her? One for you, and one for her.

"That'll be £3.50, please."

He fished out a fiver from his jacket pocket, which she put into the apron slung about her waist, and pulled out a few coins.

"There you go," she said handing him his change. "See you tomorrow."

"Or tonight?" The boy held his breath, waiting for her to respond. Instead, she looked confused. It occurred to him perhaps she was just being polite, she didn't really want to see him tomorrow, he came to see her whether she wanted him to or not.

"Tonight?" she repeated.

"Yes, I have tickets, to the theatre," he proffered the envelope, as proof. "I thought you might like to go. It's a beautiful story, by the Russian playwright Chekhov, about a girl and a boy and..."

She took the envelope from his hand and opened it.

"The Seagull," she read aloud from the ticket.

"Yes exactly!" the boy wiped his perspiring hands on his trousers under the table. "The Seagull! Do you know it? It is one of the most wonderful love stories!"

She placed the tickets down on the table again.

"Thank you, but I can't tonight I'm afraid."

"Oh," the boy tried to hide his disappointment.

"But maybe you would like to ask her?" she gestured to Anne, a woman the boy had seen many times before, who was sat alone at her table in the window. "I always see her in here reading a book, maybe she would like to go?" the girl ventured.

The boy looked from the girl with the long dark hair to the rather sad creature settled behind him, who was reading a book and had a flowery pin in her jacket lapel. He turned back to answer her, but the girl with the black hair was already gone.

\* \* \* \*

The actress had decided in the end to skip breakfast after all, and head outside into the salty seaside air. Touring had been one of her favourite parts of being a young actress, but she was no longer the ingénue, and the passage of time had eroded her love for travel. She preferred now to be at home with her beloved begonias and her brother, Trevor, who had moved in with her after his partner died. She sat on the seafront now nibbling cautiously at her punnet of chips, which were thick and yellow and scalding hot.

"They'll put me in a corset for Arkadina,' she thought to herself, debating how many more chips she could manage to eat without upsetting the costume girls.

"Best stay out of the sun too," she thought, unraveling her soft hat, which she always carried with her on days like today. "A burnt nose wouldn't do at all."

She settled back into the bench, the wood warm and comforting. She wondered if she had met this director before. It was becoming more and more difficult to remember, faces and names were becoming hazy and blank, like statues in a museum, with smooth faces and missing pieces. She wondered if he had been one of her affairs, but even the answer to this could not be dredged from her memories. She would ask Trevor on her return.

The funicular rail carriage took people up and down to the beach. The actress sat and watched with interest as the carriage juddered down the rock face. A little boy sat on his mother's knee on the bench opposite her, more ice cream on his face than in his mouth. He stared out at her unashamedly, and the actress pulled her hat a little lower. She could hear people chattering behind her, they were going to the theatre that evening, she gathered. This always gave her a glow of secret satisfaction, that they would see her tonight as the great Arkadina, and have no idea they had been sitting next to her just hours earlier, an old woman in her simple summer clothes enjoying the sunshine just like them, who did not warrant any cause for attention.

She stood up, brushed herself down and began to

make her way to the theatre. Her script was tucked into her handbag although she knew all she needed to know already. The art deco frontage of the theatre was hard to miss, and the usual smell greeted her as she walked inside, the box office empty for the morning.

The theatre itself was large and open, in the round as they called it. The director was already there, settled into his seat three rows back, a large notepad on his knee and a mug of coffee by his feet. The actors trickled in slowly, smiling and chatting with an awkward ease that comes with constantly meeting new people. The company hadn't made a visit to the theatre before, but it was easy to see whom the star was. The actress walked the whole expanse of the stage space, covering her eyes at one point to look up to the Gods.

"Beautiful space, darling," she murmured, to no one in particular.

Tonight was the first night, and although her watch told her there was still plenty of time for last minute rehearsing, she knew all too well how fast the time would tick onwards.

\*   \*   \*   \*

Above the town, Anne picked her way carefully between the shrubs, which grew around the gravestones high on the hill. Down below, the noise of holidaymakers and day-trippers drifted upwards like smoke from a cigarette, barely visible but choking none the less. She knelt down and began tending to one of the graves where wild flowers sat in pretty clustered and wasps wandered lazily between them in a summer daze. She thought how strange it was that all of life could be unfolding so closely and yet the town's dead watched on. She cleared away the last of the debris, took off her light coat and laid it onto the ground, settling onto it like a picnic rug. She opened her handbag and pulled out the last of the cake she had saved, wrapped deftly in a napkin. She balanced her tea, her third cup of the day, weak and milky, in its polystyrene cup between some stones, and unwrapped the piece of cake like a precious jewel. The harbour below stretched out languorously, the seagulls chasing each other higher and higher around the headland. She pulled out her favourite copy of 'The Tenant of Winfield Hall' and began to devour both the cake and the book with equal relish. She began to read aloud, making herself comfortable against her father's headstone. She had always lived in the town, and had always preferred it up here, away from all the people and the noise.

"Yes dad," she said to the gravestone. "When the time came, I could quite happily sit here with you forever."

\* \* \* \*

The day stretched out lazily like a cat, and at this hour the seafront belonged to those who were not from the town. The slot machines in the arcade chattered nosily to each other, with patrons hunched over them, too afraid to leave in case their diligence paid dividends. A few shouted loudly with delight as a shower of coins came flooding out. Some sat quietly, letting the sunshine soak into their city faces, lined with stress and fatigue. Their ice creams melted quickly on days like today, dripping down on fingers and making stains on sun creamed legs and summer shorts. Seagulls waddled, large and threatening, boldly mugging those who weren't careful for scraps of chips and uneaten ice cream cones.

The actress walked back out of the theatre, that familiar feeling in her stomach. The last of the afternoon sunshine was dipping downwards, and the moon had already appeared like a ghost in the blue sky. She strode downwards towards the seafront, wanting to enjoy this last part of the evening to herself.

A few streets further down, the girl with the black hair closed up the fish and chip shop, pulling the door tightly until the lock clicked into place. A few hopeful seagulls padded around her feet, until a local cat appeared with the same idea, and they chased her away instead. The local tramp, who was still lying on his bench, called her name in the darkness as she walked past him, his voice rattling with cigarettes and alcohol. The little dog that had adopted him howled dutifully from his side. The girl gave him the little parcel of leftovers from that day. The old man muttered something incomprehensible, and the girl smiled to herself and kept on walking.

The actress looked at her watch. Still plenty of time before the half, she mused. She eyed the people passing by in the dark of the evening, the young families staggering home from a day at the seaside, weighed down with buckets and spades with children slumped over their shoulders like the catches of the day. Couples followed behind, the young in tight shorts and low tops that revealed uneven white and pink skin, whilst the old came last of all, wearing a variety of hats and leaning on each other with arms entwined, shuffling upwards towards the town and a well earned dinner and bed.

Only one girl was still walking downwards. She had long black hair that snaked down her back in dry tendrils, like the rope that hung down from the boats in the harbour. Her skin was pale although she wasn't a tourist, and she walked with her eyes half closed as if her feet could take her to her destination in her sleep. She moved through the throngs of people with quiet purpose and no one seemed to notice that she was barefoot.

*   *   *   *

In the Grand Hotel, the boy was doing his last checks in one of the suites, the tight neck on his uniform scratching against the pink flesh that had been exposed by his inexperienced shaving. It was early evening; he knew the actress wouldn't be back until late. He had given his tickets for the performance tonight to Janice who worked on reception. With a sigh, he crept back up to the room to make sure everything was perfect. No one would notice him, no one ever did. The only time someone did notice him was if something wasn't perfect, then suddenly he would become all too visible to them. He took great pride in working in such a beautiful establishment, completed 1867, with its four towers to represent the four seasons, twelve floors the months, fifty-two chimneys the weeks He went to switch on the lamp by the window, and caught a glimpse of the girl with the black hair, who came to swim in the sea every evening. He wondered to himself how it was that nobody saw her, that nobody ever stopped her. Then he wondered if perhaps like him, she was invisible too. He watched her until she had disappeared from view. He looked out of the window a little longer, but nothing came back except the dusky evening light and the stillness of the seaside town.

He returned to his trolley and stocked up the side table with sachets of coffee and herbal tea, little pots of milk and prepackaged biscuits. He brushed down the bed one last time, checked that everything was in its place, and went to straighten up the curtain so that he could take one last glimpse. There was a shape now, out to sea, bobbing in the water, so small you would almost miss it.

*　*　*　*

The eyes of the actress adjusted slowly as she moved from the early evening sunshine outside to the dark of the theatre. She felt refreshed from her stroll and her nap on the bench by the sea. The costumes hung on a rail at the end, musty and heavy. Close by was the prop boxes, overflowing with samovars, old books and the pivotal dead seagull. She watched Bob shuffle past, who had been a part of the theatre as long as anyone could remember.

The stage was set for Act One, with orange blossoms entwined around the open space, the lights changing intermittently from blue to green. The other actors stood around incongruously, in corsets and shaking their hands as they walked in circles breathing loudly and making strange humming noises. She had never understood all this nonsense herself.

Instead, she settled back into one of the chairs and closed her eyes. She could still feel the heat of the sun on her eyelids and the lovely way the salty air had dried her skin and ruffled her hair. She was prepared. She had done this a thousand times before, and her muscles were poised like a tiger.

When it came time for the house lights to go down, and the stage lights to go up, her whole being fizzled with the energy of the evening.

\*     \*     \*     \*

The girl had ignored all those passing by her, and was grateful that no one had noticed her. Everyone was so blissful with the sunshine, drunk from it. She padded along the beach which was wide and flat, the houses behind were red and white and then the expanse of green which stretched out far behind. The sand was beginning to disappear, as the tide rolled in, as if the whole world were breathing deeply and each wave was a deep sigh of sleep. She walked towards the lighthouse, which stood clear, and white against the sky. The statue of the Belle stood beneath it, her arms high as if she were about to dive into the water below. Her face was smooth metal, no features to be eroded. The seagulls circled above her, as if this was her coven, a nighttime ritual.

The early evening light was fading to dusk as she walked down to the beach, the mint green railing, the colour of ice cream, gleaming in the sunset. She ran her fingers along the smooth, cold metal, and hand in hand they raced down to the sea.

The water was icy cold and she submerged herself, as fast as soon could, which always seem to help. She swam in broad strokes out until she could turn around and look back to the headland. The lights of the homes and hotels twinkled, as if they weren't real at all, as if it were just a toy town. In the distant corner, she could see Scarborough Castle, haunting and majestic. The Grand Hotel punctuated the skyline, and the dome of the Spa glinted in the light of the setting sun. She sank underneath the water again, the sound of the world disappearing into watery silence. Slowly, she kicked her way further down into the blackness of the water, and swam off as she did every evening, out into the horizon.

Scott Harrison is a scriptwriter and novelist whose stage plays have been produced in both the US and UK. He has written audio plays for a number of Big Finish ranges, including *The Confessions of Dorian Gray* and *Blake's 7: The Liberator Chronicles*, and his novel *Archangel* is the second book to be published in their new Blake's 7 novel range. His comic book scripts and short stories have appeared in a variety of anthologies, including Into *The Woods: A Fairytale Anthology* and *Faction Paradox: A Romance in Twelve Parts*. As editor he has worked on a charity eBook anthology for Great Ormond Street Hospital and is range editor for the *Modern Masters Of Audio* series. He lives on the edge of werewolf country with his wife and a stack of books he will never get around to reading.

# THE LAST TRAIN TO WHITBY

## SCOTT HARRISON

It was a little after eight in the evening when I stepped down from the train and onto the snow-covered platform.

The journey up from London had been an overly long and tedious affair; not least because I'd had to share it with some crashing bore from Pimlico by the name of Aldin. He'd climbed aboard the train somewhere outside of Stevenage, shattering all hopes I'd had of getting some peace and quiet on my long journey north.

I looked up as he bundled his way in through the door, the corner of his case banging sharply against my knees as he wrestled it into the compartment.

When his luggage had been safely stowed away in the

overhead storage rack, and he'd settled himself into the seat opposite, he offered me a cheery smile, and my heart sank.

"Edgar Aldin," he told me, extending a hand. "Eddie to my friends."

"Sanders," I replied, the old lie springing automatically to my lips. "George Sanders."

The name seemed to tickle my companion enormously. "Like the film star?"

I blew my cheeks out in feigned exasperation, offering him a smile that seemed to say: *I get that all the time!*

"I'm afraid so. It's a terrible bore sharing a name with someone famous, but there you go. You either get used to it or go mad." And I gave a little laugh, just to help the fib along.

At first I'd feigned interest in the man's polite, yet frightfully dull, chit-chat, but after more than an hour of hearing endless tales about his family and his business in central London, I found him to be quite tedious. By the time we'd reached Grantham I'd given up all pretence of playing the attentive, genial travelling companion. Instead I was watching the muddy brown fields as they rushed passed outside the train window, the sun beyond sliding slowly down the sky towards the horizon, and thinking about the telephone call I'd made earlier that morning.

I knew that Mr M-- wasn't expecting me to suddenly turn up alive, not after all this time; I could hear it in his voice the moment he'd picked up the receiver.

"Ah, there you are, my boy," Mr M-- had purred down the phone. "I was beginning to get concerned. Thought the Ruskies might have got you after all."

"How very touching," I'd replied, trying to keep the bitterness out of my voice. "I managed to get out in the end, no thanks to your contact."

There had been a pause, as though Mr M-- were weighing up my words. "The Libyan wasn't there?"

"Oh, he turned up all right; although he was about as useful as an ice-making machine in the Antarctic."

"The Papillion swears by him." Mr M-- had told me.

"Yeah? Well she won't be swearing to anything else in a hurry. The Papillion is dead!" I'd shouted, causing an old man in a long grey mac and porkpie hat to glance in through the window of the phone box as he passed. I'd decided then to lower my voice a little. "Your contact pulled a gun on us the moment we were aboard the Warsaw – Poznan express."

There had been silence on the other end of the phone for a few seconds, my words stopping Mr M-- dead in his tracks...if you'll pardon the pun.

"Oh God, I'm so sorry," he'd said at last, but I knew damn well that he wasn't. "Where's the Libyan now?"

"He got off the train somewhere outside of Kutno. Sadly it was still moving at the time."

"Well, that saves me the bother of having to deal with him, I suppose." There had been genuine amusement in the mad old bastard's voice, despite his annoyance. "You did the right thing, of course. What about the Papillion?"

"I had no choice but to leave her in the sleeper compartment. I undressed her and put her to bed, but she's probably been discovered by now."

"The Polish authorities will be all over that train with a fine-toothed comb, I trust you left nothing that would point them in our direction." Mr M-- had asked.

"Twelve years in the Department," I'd said sharply. "Have you ever known me to make such an amateurish mistake before?"

Wisely Mr M-- had decided not to answer that question. It was plain even to an old fool like him that when I was in this kind of mood it was best to just slip on the old kid gloves and try your best not to antagonise me further.

"How did you make it across the border?" he'd asked.

"Used my initiative," I'd said. "Just like you taught me."

"So, where do you go from here?" Mr M-- had asked me then, probably knowing full well that I wasn't going to give him a straight answer. To tell the truth, I had absolutely no idea what I was going to do now, and wouldn't have told Mr M-- even if I *had* known.

First rule of obstacle removal – never let them know when you're coming.

"I really don't know. Not back to London, that's for sure. I don't think either of us is quite ready for that just yet. I'm going to catch a train this afternoon, haven't decided which yet..."

Someone coughed and my eyes darted away from the window, towards my companion on the seat opposite. This frightful chap, Aldin, had finally stopped talking, and was now looking at me with a somewhat peculiar expression.

"I say, are you all right? You don't look at all well if you ask me. Your face is frightfully pale." His concern seemed quite genuine.

At first I said nothing, instead I passed the palm of one hand across my forehead and it came back wet and clammy. In the train window my face seemed unnaturally round and bone white, like a winter moon; splinters of black shadow rested in the hollows beneath my eyes, giving me a vaguely zombic air.

"No, I'm fine," I said, finding my voice at last. "Feeling a little under the weather this evening, that's all."

Not exactly the whole truth, but it did the trick. My companion seemed more than satisfied with my explanation, prompting him to lift the folded newspaper from his lap and tap at the front page. The headline read FLU EPIDEMIC LOOMS LARGE.

"Perhaps it's a touch of flu. According to the broadsheets this is only the beginning. Most of the country's going to be hit for six by it," Aldin seemed to take great delight in telling me this. "If it wasn't for this damn business up north I'd be locking myself indoors and waiting for it to burn itself out."

"I'm sure we'll be fine, in the end." I said.

He smiled at that, saying, "If you say so, old boy. If you say so."

* * *

I decided to kill Edgar Aldin just before we pulled into Whitby station. I stepped up behind him as he stood to retrieve his luggage and snapped his neck cleanly, before he had the opportunity to cry out. I made a quick search through his pockets, but found nothing that connected him with either Mr M-- or the Department, so I bundled his body into the toilet cubicle and jammed the lock.

I stepped from the train with Aldin's cards and identification papers stuffed inside my jacket, and made my way slowly and calmly towards the exit. At the end of the platform a young man in a British Railways uniform punched my ticket and wished me a pleasant stay, before turning and repeating the procedure with the lady behind.

I stood at the top of the steps by the mouth of the station, my back against one of the brick pillars, staring up at the crumbling ruins of the Abbey, and tried not to think about the dead man I'd left on the train.

I'd been so sure that Aldin was one of Mr M--'s goons sent to shadow me on the journey; put there to find out where I was going, who I was meeting, then report back. Maybe even remove me, if Mr M-- deemed it necessary.

But the man had been totally clean; no gun or service card, nothing.

It was somewhat ironic that I'd spent my first few moments in Whitby murdering an innocent man, seeing as that's how I'd spent my final moments here, all those years ago.

Twelve years, that's how long it had been, and I'd swore to myself then that I'd never come back. Wasn't it bad enough that I spent every night listening to the man pleading for his life over and over, without putting myself through the indignity of all this again, and risk making it a hundred times worse?

The last time I'd been here (the time when I'd put a bullet through someone's head) was at the end of the war; either late July or early August, not sure which. A few weeks after, the Japs finally surrendered and we all celebrated VJ Day, so I guess you can figure out the dates yourself if you want to. It really doesn't matter what the date had been, all I know is it was damned hot; so hot the tar in the roads had become soft and tacky underfoot, and the air above the pavement by the harbour had shimmered like smoke in the mid-afternoon sun.

I reached into my pocket, looking for a packet of cigarettes, and my hand brushed against the gun holstered beneath my arm. It was the same gun, the very same one that had killed that man down on Tate Hill Beach all those years ago. Only back then, inexperience had made the weapon feel clumsy and awkward in my hands, the weight of the barrel just that little bit too heavy as I tried to aim it, its kick so violent that it made my arm tingle right up to the shoulder...

"You just got in?"

The voice took me by surprise, shattering those dry and brittle memories into a thousand jagged pieces. I looked down to find a girl hovering at the bottom of the steps. She was standing with her back to the street lamp, shadows across her face, hair circling her head like a ring of luminous vapour. From what I could see of her she looked quite young; late teens / early twenties perhaps, certainly no older than that. Pretty too, in an unremarkable sort of a way.

"Just this minute." I told her, jerking a thumb towards the train

"Stranger in a strange land, eh?" She said, and giggled.

I shrugged. "Something like that."

"And on such a cold night, too. You'll catch your death."

"I'm up here for a few days on business. My name's Aldin. Edgar Aldin, but my friends call me Eddie."

"All on your own are you, Eddie?"

I nodded.

"Have you sorted yourself out a place to stay yet?"

This time I shook my head.

"My mum runs a bed and breakfast called *The Sandpiper's Rest,* it's over that way." She pointed across the harbour, towards the east side of the town. "You know it?"

"Can't say I do, no," I said, playing the stranger card to the hilt. "Is she cheap, your mum?"

The ghost of a smile fluttered across her lips. "Better not let her hear you ask that, or she'll have your guts for garters."

So I grabbed my suitcase and we wandered off through the frozen streets, towards the little metal swing bridge that would takes us across the water to the opposite side of the town.

* * *

*I've got the man by the scruff of the neck and I'm
dragging him along Tate Hill Pier, down the short flight
of stone steps and onto the small semi-circle of beach.
He's kicking and screaming and pleading for his life,
but it doesn't make any difference. He has to die, it's as
simple as that. I knock his legs out from under him and
he goes down onto his knees. I pull the gun out then,
aiming it at the base of his skull, and this is where he
tells me about his wife, about his little girl. I look up and
see the woman half-hidden in the dark, standing over by
the rocks a little way off, crying as she holds on to her
daughter, begging me to spare her husband's life. For a
moment I hesitate - not long, just four or five seconds -
then I squeeze the trigger. The gun kicks in my hand and
a plume of blood is spraying into the air; it lands on my
face, my clothes, coats the wet sand at my feet. And out
there in the dark the child is screaming and screaming...*

* * *

I awoke the next morning to the sounds of the seagulls
screeching and squawking on the sloping roof beneath my
window, and I opened my eyes to discover that the sun
was already up. I threw the covers to one side, swinging

my legs out of bed, and reached for the pack of smokes and lighter on the bedside table.

The bed and breakfast had been as small and as nondescript as I'd hoped it would be; a crooked little building tucked away in a crooked little court off the crooked little market square. I'd gone in and picked up my key, then popped up to the room just long enough to dump my suitcase on the bed and transfer Aldin's cards and driver's licence to my wallet. Then I'd gone back downstairs where I'd found the girl waiting for me by the front desk...

After that, things got a little hazy.

I half-remember the girl's arm around my shoulders as she helped me out of the *Duke of York* pub an hour or two later - the cold night air hitting me like a good back-hander across the chops - then being violently sick in a narrow little alleyway down by the harbour. We must have made it back to the bed and breakfast soon afterwards, because I had vague recollections of pulling the girl roughly towards me and making clumsy, impatient grabbing motions at her breasts as she unbuttoned her blouse. It was followed by a rather embarrassing and unsuccessful attempt at making love.

Then I don't remember anything.

Except for the dreams, of course.

Behind me the girl began to stir softly as I flipped the

top of the Zippo and lit a cigarette. She lay there silently for a little while, just watching me; I could feel her cold blue eyes boring into the back of my head.

I tossed the lighter back onto the table, where it clattered across the wooden surface like machine gun fire, disturbing the silence.

"Are you a policeman?" she asked suddenly.

It wasn't the question I was expecting, and I turned around on the bed so I could look her full in the face. This early in the morning, woman like her usually asked questions like "So, are you married?" or "Am I going to get to see you again?". Never before have I been asked if I was a copper.

I shook my head. "Why'd you ask?"

The girl pointed across at the wooden chair in the opposite corner of the room and the holstered gun hanging from one of the arms. "Only policemen and bank robbers carry guns, don't they? At least, they do in all those Yankie films."

"Maybe they do in America, but not here," I said. "I'm not a copper and I certainly don't stick guns into bank clerk's faces."

"What do you need that for, then?" she asked.

I pulled myself up off the bed and padded across the room to the crumpled pile of clothes over by the chair.

"It's for protection, mostly. But sometimes I use it for my work."

"Are you someone important?"

I couldn't help but laugh. "What, like a movie star, you mean?"

"Well, maybe not a movie star, but you could be connected to the government." She said.

"Do I look like Anthony Eden, love?"

"Who's Anthony Eden?"

I turned and stared at her in silence, trying to figure out whether she was being serious or just pulling my leg. At last I said, "How old *are* you?"

She straightened herself up a little then, all indignant-like; as though my question had been intended as an insult – which in a way it was. "I'll be eighteen in four months' time. But I don't see what that's got to do with it."

Bending over, I scooped my shirt off the floor and slipped my arms into the sleeves. "Because an adult would know the name of our bloody Prime Minister, that's what it's got to do with it." I said, coldly. "If I'd have known you were still wet behind the ears I wouldn't have fucked you last night."

"You *couldn't* fuck me last night, that was the problem." She hesitated a moment, as though regretting her words. Then – "Have you ever killed someone?"

When I didn't answer her straight away, she pulled herself up into a sitting position on the bed, and pointed once more at the gun hanging on the chair.

"With that thing, I mean. Have you ever used it on a man - shot him dead?"

Somehow her question made me feel uneasy, as though the answer was incredibly important to her. I made a show of buttoning up my shirt, slowly and carefully, then tucking it into my trousers, before turning to look at her.

"Sometimes, when I'm asked to and it's necessary," I explained.

"Have you ever been asked when it's unnecessary?"

I turned away, refusing to answer, continuing to dress in silence.

Just before I left the room, the girl asked if she could see me again. I told her I'd think about it and closed the door behind me.

\* \* \*

There were one hundred and ninety-nine steps in all. I remembered that from the last time I was here, and I counted them off under my breath as I went.

Between the houses away to my left I could see Tate Hill Pier and the small semi-circular stretch of beach disappearing off towards the mouth of the harbour, and just for a second last night's dream jolted through my head like an electrical current...

*(No, no, please, don't kill me, not in front of my daughter. She's only five years old. Please, spare her the sight of that.)*

...and I stopped and turned to look at the view. I was only half way up, but already I could see as far as the old stone viaduct away to my left, the smooth grey ribbon of the River Esk beneath it, snaking its way through the centre of the town and disappearing inland. To my right the sea was dark and brooding, like one vast strip of sheet metal, its surface dappled here and there by foaming white horse that broke suddenly upon reaching the walls of the harbour.

The man was waiting for me at the top of the steps. I recognised him for what he was immediately; practically unmistakable in winged collar shirt, cream suit and matching Panama. He was sitting on a bench in St. Mary's Church graveyard and watching the fishing boats chugging merrily out to sea.

"Don't blame me," he said without taking his eyes off the view in front of him. "I'm here on Mr M--'s instructions."

"I don't need a nurse maid." I told him.

"Look on me as your Guardian Angel then, if that helps." He said, with a grin.

I stopped next to the bench, but refused to sit down, jamming the last of the cigarettes between my lips and tossing the empty packet onto the grass. "I really don't care what you want me to call you, I don't want you here. Mr M-- knows that."

The man turned his face towards me, the remains of a grin still tugging at the corners of his mouth. He thrust a hand out for me to shake. "The Count."

I laughed, despite myself. "What sort of a codename is that?"

"Mr M-- thought it might be appropriate," the Count said, waving a hand at our surroundings. "With it being Whitby, and all that."

"So what name have I been assigned? Harker, perhaps? Or Van Helsing?"

The grin on the Count's face suddenly grew more pronounced. "Demeter."

"Wonderful," I said. "You get the title role and I get named after the boat."

"I came up with the names myself, I'm rather pleased with them." The Count seemed genuinely delighted.

"Makes no difference to me what you choose to call either of us, I don't want you here."

"That's a pity, because I've been given orders to stay here and keep an eye on you."

"Why?" I asked.

With the tip of a finger the Count pushed the brim of his Panama backwards so that he could watch the seagulls swoop and soar above the old church tower. He sat in contemplative mood like this for a few moments, before deciding to answer my question.

"After your recent escapades in the U.S.S.R, I rather think that Mr M-- is concerned for your mental well-being."

"That's nice of him," I said, drily.

"Well, you know Mr M--, he's nothing if not thoughtful."

"Does he think I'm going to strip off one morning and go rushing out into the sea?" I asked him.

The Count glanced furtively down at my jacket, just beneath my left arm, where the gun was holstered. "I think his concerns are more for the safety of others."

"I've come out of trickier situations than this before and he's never sent a wet nurse to watch over me. Why now?"

The Count looked up at me suddenly, his eyes wide and flashing. "The Papillion's death. Mr M-- believes that you might be blaming yourself."

All these years he must have known about our...

relationship. Even though we kept it a secret from our respective governments, thinking that if they ever found out we'd be arrested as traitors, probably even shot. And all this time Mr M-- had known. So, the old bastard was much cleverer than I had given him credit for.

I shrugged, pretending that the whole thing meant nothing to me. "People die in this business every day, most of them by my hand; it's what I'm paid for. If there's an obstacle in the way, I remove it – permanently. The Libyan had a similar job. I guess the Papillion was the obstacle he was hired to remove, that's how things go sometimes."

"I think it's the 'permanent removal' aspect of your job that's particularly concerning Mr M--."

There was something in the Count's tone that I didn't quite care for, a sort of latent menace. "What's that supposed to mean?"

"Well, you were a little...abrupt with him on the phone, weren't you?"

I felt the colour suddenly drain from my face. "Mr M-- thinks I'm going to try and kill him?"

"It did cross his mind."

"That's absurd." I told him.

"So you're not angry with him? This Papillion's death means nothing to you?" The Count asked.

I shook my head. "Not especially."

He must have known that I wasn't telling him the truth, because he said, "And yet after such a traumatic experience you came back here. Don't you find that interesting?"

I looked at him for a moment, trying to figure out just how much Mr M-- had told him about my past. "Why the hell should I?"

"This being the place where – using your euphemism - you *removed* your first obstacle," he said. "Your first traumatic experience in the Department, so I'm told."

"Did Mr M-- tell you all this?" I asked, my voice more than a little shaky.

The grin was back once more, fluttering across his lips like a swarm of summer butterflies, and for the first time I noticed just how thin and red they really were. 'The Count' was an apt name, indeed. "Some of it, the rest I read in your file before I came. I like to know all about the people I'm...looking after. I like to get to know them until I feel as though they were my own flesh and blood, as it were. Only that way can I really do my job to its fullest." That menacing tone was back.

"Did Mr M--- happen to mention that the guy was a nobody? Did he? Did he explain how the Department wasn't sure if I had what it takes, so it set up a little test, just for me, down there on that beach? Did he tell you that?"

The Count appeared untroubled by my discomfort and went back to watching the seagulls wheeling overhead.

"Those are the prices one has to pay in order to work for the Department, Demeter," he said at last. "If they had deemed it necessary to put you to the test, then so be it."

I shook my head violently. "The man was a local, completely uninvolved. He had a wife and a child – a daughter."

The Count stared at me for a second or two, then jumped briskly to his feet (and it was then that I noticed just how small the chap really was; five-one or five-two, certainly no more than that). "Yes, she was very young, just five years old. I am well aware of the facts; they were all there in your file."

"I had to shoot him in front of the girl, in front of his wife, too. He's responsible for all this…" And I flapped my hands vaguely around me. "He's responsible for what I have become today."

The little man's eyes narrowed as he regarded me in the pale morning light. Then he said, "Yet you happily pulled the trigger, all those years ago. Even though you knew what the Department was asking you to do. What does that say about you, Demeter? Who do you think is really responsible for the man you are today?"

I turned my back on him and started to walk away. I

hadn't gone more than five paces when the Count called out from somewhere behind me.

"Be a smart man, Demeter, and stay in Whitby for a while. I'll be sticking around to make sure you cool off a little. Maybe then Mr M-- will allow you to come back to the Department. Who knows, maybe in time we can all sit down and discuss the matter sensibly like adults."

\* \* \*

The Count had been sent to kill me. I knew that the moment I left the churchyard and descended the one hundred and ninety-nine steps to the east side of town.

All this talk of the Count being sent here out of thoughtful concern was just bullshit. What it really came down to was that a Department agent was pissed off by the way he'd been treated and Mr M-- was desperately trying to cover his own back.

It wasn't the first time this had happened, either.

Back in '48, the Department had sent a scalphunter out to North Africa to stir up trouble amongst the local guerrilla armies; the idea being that a small, local war would seriously disrupt all Soviet military activity there. For a short while, at any rate. Forty-eight hours into his mission, the 'hunter, codenamed Neptune, had been captured crossing the Algerian / Tunisian border and handed over to the Soviets for interrogation.

It comes as no surprise, then, to learn that the Department had closed the file on Neptune the moment the news of his capture had reached its collective ears, officially classifying him as Missing Presumed Dead. Nearly eighteen months later, reports that Neptune had resurfaced in a sanatorium in Budapest called the *Hospital of St Joseph and Ste Mary*, sparked fears that the scalphunter was on his way back to England and gunning for the four heads of the Department.

A group of jackals had immediately been released to stop the man before he had a chance to get back into the country. Issuing the order for his termination had been the newly promoted Head of Operations, Mr M--, who had personally given them cart blanche to use 'all and any such force deemed necessary' to stop the rogue agent from making it back to London.

Neptune had managed to get all the way to Le Man in France before he met a rather eccentric little man in a cream suit and matching Panama hat. He'd been killed by a single, efficient bullet to the back of the head (the Department's calling card), his pockets filled with rocks, and his body thrown in the Sarthe River.

That's how any agent who feels that they have a

grievance with the Department is dealt with, and it would seem that I was no different.

It appeared that the only way I could get out of this alive was to deal with the Count first. Or, to put it another way – remove him, before he removed me.

*　*　*

The cosh, when it struck, took me completely by surprise, catching me a good one right across the top of my shoulders; hard enough to stun me, but not knock me out completely, which was the whole idea. Whoever had delivered the blow wanted me conscious and lucid, rather than sleeping like a baby for the next two hours.

He must have been hiding behind the door as I walked in, but with the curtains closed the whole room was still in semi-darkness and I didn't see a thing until it was too late. I fell awkwardly, like a sack of King Edwards, my head connecting sharply with the corner of the wooden chair. Fireworks exploded across my vision, and just for a moment I was no longer in a tiny room, in a tiny bed and breakfast, in a tiny fishing village on the North Yorkshire coast, but back in that hotel room in London last New Year's Eve, standing at the window with the Papillion, watching the rockets explode over the water and the

Catherine Wheels spitting their bright yellow circles of fire and sparks along the riverbank.

I felt rough hands grabbing at my shoulders, and I was lifted off the floor and dragged backwards out of the room and down the stairs.

Outside the daylight was like an interrogator's lamp in the face, sudden and brutal and very, very painful. Then I heard a car door open and I was quickly pushed inside.

I'm not sure where I was taken, although it must have been a place somewhere on the west side of the town, because at one point I could hear that rumbling-crunching sound that a car tire makes as it passes across the rough tarmacadamed surface of the swing bridge.

When the car finally stopped, I was manhandled back out into the fresh air and into another building – only this time instead of going upstairs, I was dragged down a short flight of stone steps that widened out at the bottom into a large basement room, before being dropped onto the floor.

It was bitterly cold down here, much colder than the frozen streets above, as though this were some kind of huge refrigeration unit beneath a butcher's shop. I looked up, half expecting to see the pale, almost colour-less grey carcasses of cows and sheep hanging down from great hooks in the ceiling. But there were none.

There was only the grinning diminutive form of the Count.

The young girl was standing at his side, hands clasped behind her back.

"I believe you two have already met," the Count said, smiling somewhat lasciviously. "So there's no need for me to make formal introductions."

I dragged myself painfully into a kneeling position, rubbing a careful hand across the sore spot between my shoulder blades. "You didn't waste much time. I was hoping that you might give me thirty minutes head start." My eyes flicked across to the girl. "So who are you then? His daughter?"

The Count chuckled softly to himself, then he threw a hand around the girl's shoulders and pulled her to him. "Oh, no, no! She's not *my* daughter, but she is *someone's* daughter!"

I was starting to get pins and needles in my feet now, so I shifted somewhat gingerly onto my backside, stretching my legs out in front of me. "We're all *someone's* sons and daughters; you included Count – even if the legality of your parents' marriage is currently in question."

"Such a Wildean wit you have, Demeter," the Count said. "But the father of this girl isn't just anyone – oh, no, no! He's someone you once knew rather well…albeit very briefly."

The girl stepped forward then, swinging the gun up from behind her back and training it on me. She was bearing her teeth in such an odd, almost primordial way, that it took me a second or two to realise that she wasn't actually grinning, but clenching her teeth in concentration.

"It was you – you're the one that killed him," the girl spat the words out at me as though it were a curse. "All these years I've been waiting for this day, *dreaming* about it, and here you are - the man who killed my father."

I knew that I had to play this one just right or I was a dead man.

Slowly I turned to the Count and said, "What did you tell her?"

"Just the truth. Although, to be fair, she'd all but worked it out for herself. Clever girl, this one."

I turned back to the girl and raised my hands, palms outwards, to show her that I was sorry. "It was nothing personal against your father; I was just doing as I was instructed."

The Count nodded at these words. "That is true."

"I didn't know he was an innocent man when I killed him." I said.

This time the Count shook his head. "That is most definitely *not* true."

I nodded enthusiastically towards the small figure in off white standing nearby, and then began to tremble in terror – just a little bit, you understand; I didn't want to over-do it. "It was him, he chose the target, he was the one who instructed me to kill your father."

The Count's eyes widened a little as the full understanding of my words hit home. "What are you saying, Demeter? Don't listen to him, he knew that your father was an innocent man and killed him willingly."

The gun wavered in the girl's hand and I knew that if I pushed hard enough now I might be able to turn this situation around. But if I was going to make this convincing enough for the girl to really buy it, then I'd have to twist and grovel like a coward, to give her my best impersonation of the kicked and beaten animal she wanted – or rather expected - me to be.

"Tell her," I whimpered pathetically. "Go on; tell her how you threatened her mother. Tell her that I had no choice."

The girl spun on the spot, swinging the gun around so that it now pointed directly at the Count's temple.

"He... he's lying," the Count spluttered. "Don't listen to him."

I was up on my knees again, hands clasped together

as though pleading for my life, and nodding ever more enthusiastically. "I didn't want to do, but he said that if I didn't the Department would kill you all – you, your father, your mother, all of you. Do you see the choice I was given?"

The girl's finger tightened on the trigger as she gripped the handle with both hands, desperately trying to stop the gun from shaking.

"Demeter, stop this now." The Count warned. And for the first time in his life I really think the little bastard was starting to get scared.

"Either I killed your father, or the Count killed all three of you. What could I do but obey?"

And just then I knew exactly what I had to say.

"Let's take him down to Tate Hill Beach, make him pay for what he made me do to your father!"

\* \* \*

It was a little after four in the afternoon when I stepped down from the train and onto the snow-covered platform.

The journey up to London had been an overly long and tedious affair; not least because I'd had to share it with a rather boring couple from Hull by the name of Mr and Mrs Stanhope. They'd climbed aboard the train somewhere outside of Doncaster, shattering all hopes I'd had of getting some peace and quiet on my long journey south.

I looked up as they bundled their way in through the door, the corner of a suitcase banging sharply against my knees as they wrestled themselves, one at a time, into the compartment.

When their entire luggage had been safely stowed away in the overhead storage rack, and they'd settled themselves into the seats opposite, the man offered me a cheery smile, and my heart sank.

"Charles Stanhope," he told me, extending a hand. "And this is my wife, Dulcie."

"Sanders," I replied, the old lie springing automatically to my lips. "George Sanders."

The name seemed to tickle my companions enormously.

"Like the film star?" Mrs Stanhope asked, delightedly.

I blew my cheeks out in feigned exasperation, offering them a smile that seemed to say: *I get that all the time!*

"I'm afraid so. It's a terrible bore sharing a name with someone famous, but there you go. You either get used to it or you go mad, I'm afraid." And I gave a little laugh, just to help the fib along.

At first I'd feigned interest in the couple's polite, yet frightfully dull, chit-chat, but after more than an hour of hearing endless tales about their family and friends, not to mention his business in Sheffield, I found them both to be quite tedious. By the time we'd reached Grantham I'd given up all pretence of playing the attentive, genial travelling companion. Instead I was watching the muddy brown fields as they rushed passed outside the train window, the sun beyond sliding slowly down the sky towards the horizon, and thinking about the two bodies I'd thrown over the cliffs near Whitby Abbey.

It would be a good twelve hours before they were washed ashore, another day or so before it made the national papers.

There'll be plenty of time to get to Mr M-- before then.

I'll kill him in his office; probably make his secretary watch while I do it, too. A single, efficient bullet to the back of the head – the Department's calling card.

And then I'll catch a train. I don't know which one yet, I haven't decided.

Not that it really matters. Not anymore.

Trevor Baxendale has written Doctor Who and Torchwood novels for BBC Books, including *Eater of Wasps, The Undertaker's Gift, The Deadstone Memorial* and *Prisoner of the Daleks*. His novel *Fear of the Dark* was reprinted in 2013 as part of Doctor Who's 50th Anniversary celebrations. He has also written scripts for Big Finish's *Doctor Who, Robin Hood* and *Highlander* audio plays, as well as writing various adaptations for schools in Pearsons *Bugclub* range. He has been a regular visitor to both Scarborough and Whitby with his family for many years. Follow him on Twitter at @trevorbaxendale

# THE WOMAN IN THE SAND

## TREVOR BAXENDALE

Kate closed her eyes slowly.

It wasn't especially hot today, in fact there was quite a bit of cloud, but if she relaxed she could feel the warmth of the sun on her face. There was a breeze, coming off the sea, but it wasn't cold. It was strong enough to play with the hair that hadn't been caught in her pony tail though. The hair stroked her skin.

Her sandals were off; the sand was skin-warm beneath the soles of her feet. If she dug her toes in she could feel the grittiness between them. An old, familiar feeling.

'Mum? Can I go down to the sea?'

Kate opened one eye, just a crack, because it was very

bright. 'Sure. But be careful. Don't go where I can't see you.'

'Kay.' Tom scampered away, hurrying over the dregs of seaweed and puddles of cold water. His bare feet patted quickly down to the water's edge and splashed happily. Kate closed her eye again, but it wasn't the same now, she couldn't relax. She could hear the other people on the beach – the kids playing, screaming, laughing, adults calling to them, and there was no way she could keep track of Tom now with her eyes closed.

She sat up in the deck chair, shielding her eyes with one hand while she watched him play in the surf. The sea was shallow, safe, clean. Kate had come to Scarborough every year with her parents when she was a child, almost from birth, right up until she was fourteen, and it had never really changed. Her own son, Tom, was nearly eight and this was the first time he'd ever been to a beach. Kate felt ashamed, as if she had let him down. There hadn't really been the time or opportunity before now, but since Tom's father had left... Kate had wanted a change, *needed* a change, and a break from foreign holidays. Florida, Mexico, the Maldives... they had been great, but they were expensive. And it wasn't just the money. She needed some kind of reconnection with her past. Something safe and familiar and happy.

So, Scarborough.

They'd come by train and stayed in a hotel. Tom was ecstatic. Like all children, he felt the beach's immediate claim on his heart and soul: donkey rides, sand castles, digging, running, jumping and splashing and gasping in the cold waves. He'd run up and down the beach in excitement at the sight of the little pirate boat as it sailed out across the bay every fifteen minutes. Eventually, when he was too cold to continue and his fingers and toes were almost blue, Kate had towelled him dry and he'd put his T-shirt and shorts back on and squeezed his sandy feet back into the new flip-flops they'd bought from one of the sea front shops. Then they had walked along the front, buying hot, sugary donuts from the kiosk by the RNLI station. Tired but happy, Tom had marvelled at the lights and sounds coming from the arcades as they sauntered all the way to the tiny fairground at the start of the pier.

'Can we go in?' Tom asked.

'In a couple of days. We'll save it for near the end.'

They stood and watched the twister and the big wheel for a while and then moved on. They browsed in the Shell Shack and then wandered back eating ice creams. There was a bit of a wind getting up now, but they didn't care.

They went for a ride on the pirate boat: Tom had kneeled up on the bench and peered over the edge for the whole time, waving madly at the people on the pier and on the beach, laughing as the wind caught up some sea spray and flicked it playfully over them. Kate smiled and listened to the quiet drone of the sea-shanties and the engine and wished the trip would never end.

Back on dry land, the smell of the fishing boats in their nostrils, and the taste of salt on their lips, Kate and Tom started the long walk back along the front to where they started.

On the way they came across a group of men making sand sculptures. They were positioned by the railings, so that people could stop as they walked past and lean over to admire their handiwork. It also allowed the sculptors as long as possible before the tide reached them. Even now it was only a hundred metres or so away, frothing and burbling gently as the day came to an end and the sea reclaimed the beach. There were a few people still left, packing up or drying their kids or just enjoying a last walk along the shore. But the sculptors were getting quite a crowd.

There were some surprisingly intricate shapes carved into the damp sand: sea horses and dolphins were favoured by one of the artists. The creatures were set out in a wide milieu, and looked to be dancing amid fronds of carefully defined seaweed. Kate and Tom marvelled at the detail and the skill that must have been required. The man responsible, a muscular black guy in a vest and cargo trousers, was sitting on a stool smiling broadly at the passers-by as they tossed coins into a bucket next to him.

A little further along the front was a long, languorous mermaid, her sandy hair artfully covering her breasts. The mounds that represented her chest had been carefully, and generously, realised in the sand. This had been drawn – if that was the right word – by a man with hair as long as the mermaid's, but tied back in a bright pirate bandana. He was whip-thin and surprisingly pale, even though he was stripped to the waist. He had an array of tools laid out in the sand by his feet – spades, along with spatulas and brushes, a watering can and even a water-pistol. It took ingenuity as well as artistry to create these sand sculptures, Kate realised.

There was a spectacular lifeboat, complete with portholes and ropes, surging through the ocean. It was more crudely sculptured than the mermaid and the sea creatures, but it had a dramatic life of its own and had been drawn – or carved, whatever – by a father and son team. The boy looked to be around fourteen and Kate could see Tom watching him carefully as he worked. They used sand dug from a trench beneath the image, and there was a bucket of water close by. The father was using a collection of plastic spades to do the bulk of the work.

Kate watched them work for a while and then, with a start, realised that Tom was no longer by her side.

Glancing along the front, she saw him leaning on the rail a bit further along, on his own, admiring another sculpture in the sand.

This one had gone almost unnoticed by the rest of the crowd. It was a lot more lifelike than the others – a beautiful woman, lying in the sand as if she was sunbathing. She wasn't a mermaid; her long, lovely legs stretched almost all the way to the wall at Tom's feet. She was perfectly proportioned, almost a goddess. Kate thought the sculpture was utterly breath-taking. It was all in the eyes, she realised. They were just made from sand, but they seemed to stare back up off the beach at Kate, almost following her like the eyes of a portrait.

The man responsible for the sunbathing beauty was sitting nearby. His hair was tousled and fair – sandy, thought Kate, mischievously – and his skin was sunburned, the colour of milky coffee and he wore tan shorts and T-shirt and old, comfortable sandals. He could have been made from sand himself.

He looked up at Kate with tawny eyes and smiled.

'She's beautiful,' Kate said, without really knowing why she said it.

'Thanks,' he replied. He glanced down at the woman in the sand. 'I like to think so.'

'It must have taken you ages.'

He shrugged. 'I'm a quick worker. You have to be

with sand. Go too slow and it dries out and you can't do anything with it.'

Kate smiled, intrigued. There didn't seem to be any of the usual paraphernalia around – no spades, knives, spatulas, brushes or water. He didn't even have a stool to sit on or a bucket or cloth to catch donations from passers-by.

'Have you been doing this long?' she asked.

'Yep,' he said with a nod. 'I've been here longer than any of the others, that's for sure.'

'Was it all done by hand?'

'Yep.'

'You're very talented.'

'Thanks.'

Kate and Tom had this man to themselves. Everyone else was still captivated by the sculptors further up the beach. Trust Tom to find this gem, thought Kate.

'What do you do when the tide comes in?' Tom asked the man. 'It'll all get washed away.'

The man shrugged and smiled. 'I'll still be here,' he said.

When it was time to move on, Kate smiled back at the man and said goodnight. He watched her put her arm around Tom as she led him away. He was excited and full of questions.

'Why doesn't he build sand castles?' he wanted to

know as they made their way back towards the hotel. 'If I was as good an artist as that, I wouldn't waste my time making girls in the sand. I'd make sand castles. Big ones! With moats and drawbridges and everything. I bet he could do it.'

'Yes,' agreed Kate. 'I bet he could.'

* * * *

Next day, they did all the same things again, although they didn't do the pirate boat. Kate took Tom straight on to the fair instead, a wild, giddy rush from the twisters to the dodgems and everything in between. It cost Kate a small fortune, but it was worth it – Tom hardly stopped laughing for two hours solid, and Kate herself felt like a girl again. Tom ate candy floss for the first time in his life. They had their lunch on the beach and watched the people swimming and splashing in the surf for a while as they got their breath back. At the end of the day they walked back along the front.

Luckily the man was there again with his sand sculptures. Kate hoped he would be. She wanted to see him again, and Tom was excited to see the carvings in the sand. He had tried his own during the afternoon, but even with Kate's help the results were rudimentary to say at best.

Oddly, none of the other sand artists were here today. One or two people slowed to look at what the man had made in the sand, but few stopped. Kate and Tom watched him over the rail again as the sun sank slowly towards the horizon.

The woman was there again, in the sand. Naked, beautiful, alluring, somehow familiar. Her sand eyes watched Kate very carefully, or so it seemed.

'Why don't you build sand castles?' Tom asked.

The man smiled up at him. He was wearing the same dusty clothes as yesterday. Nothing had changed, Kate was glad to note. She glanced at the woman in the sand. She was still looking at Kate.

'I bet they'd be brilliant,' Tom said, 'if you built sand castles.' He climbed through the railings and jumped down onto the beach with his bucket and spade. The man watched, amused, as the boy took a place a few yards away and began to fill his bucket.

'He's full of life,' the man said to Kate.

'Yes. He'll wear me out one day.'

They watched Tom play for a minute and then Kate asked, 'Is it someone you know?' She was pointing at the woman in the sand.

The man studied the effigy for a few seconds and then shrugged. 'Maybe – once. Or maybe I will know her. Maybe it's who I'm looking for.'

'She looks so real,' Kate remarked. 'Almost familiar –
maybe I've seen her around here?'

The man smiled sadly. 'Maybe. Lots of people come
to Scarborough.' He looked back up a Kate and added,
'Some never leave.'

'Did you come to Scarborough? Or where you born and
bred here?'

'Yes, I came here a long, long time ago. As near born
and bred as anything, I suppose. I'll never leave. Not until
I've found her, anyway...' He nodded at the woman in the
sand.

Kate thought the conversation was getting a bit
peculiar now, so she decided it was time to move on.
She called to Tom that it was time to go. Reluctantly he
picked up his bucket and spade and trudged up the beach,
leaving a little village of lop-sided castles behind him.

'See you tomorrow?' asked the man as they said
goodbye. Kate felt her chest tighten a little.

'Yes, maybe,' she said.

\*    \*    \*    \*

That night Kate had a nightmare. She didn't dream
often, and nightmares were rare. But this was a full on
horror story. Tom slept quietly through it all, thankfully,
but Kate woke up with a jerk and a gasp thinking she

was being buried alive in the sand. She lay on the bed, panting, for a full minute before she got up and went to the bathroom. Her mouth was sand-dry. She drank some tap water and spat it out. There was grit in it. She brushed her teeth and climbed back into bed with the lingering sense of suffocation and a terrible thirst.

\*　\*　\*　\*

They stayed on the beach the next day. It was beautiful, warm and sunny. Kate was very tired, but Tom was happier than she could remember seeing him for a long time. He dug holes in the sand, built sand castles, and managed to cajole Kate into burying him. She wasn't keen on the idea after last night's bad dream, but he seemed so excited and was practically begging her. He had even dug a large enough hole himself and so she helped cover him in loose sand – only up to his chest, with him lying down. She piled loose sand up around his shoulders until only his head could be seen as he giggled.

No sooner had she finished than he burst out again, laughing hysterically. She chased him down to the water's edge and they splashed about for an hour before returning, soaked and happy, to their spot. They had their sandwiches and tea from a flask, and Tom sat and read his comic for a while. Kate watched the people around them. It was nearly the end of the holiday season and the crowds had thinned out a lot. Eventually she dozed off, her face warmed by the sun as she sat back in the hired deck chair.

She woke up slowly, feeling relaxed and rested. She didn't know how long she had slept because her watch was still in her bag, but the tide had come quite a bit. When she had closed her eyes the surf had been two hundred yards away, now if was no more than fifty. It was also slightly chillier; there were a lot more clouds in the sky and some of them were quite grey.

There was no sign of Tom.

She felt an immediate stab of fear deep in her stomach. She sat up, looking hurriedly all around the beach. He wasn't by the deck chair, or his sand castles, or anywhere near her. There were a few people around, but no sign of her boy. Panic held her for a moment – until she spotted him, finally, a hundred yards away.

He was playing with the sand man at the water's edge.

Kate drew a deep breath and calmed herself down. The initial fear had gone, but she felt a confusion of relief and anger deep inside. Her heart was pounding.

And what was he doing with the sand man? Why was the sand man even *here*?

Tom was looking back at her now, smiling broadly,

completely relaxed. The sand man, tall and tanned, waved at her.

Kate squirmed in her deck chair. She wasn't entirely comfortable with this. She wanted to stand up, to stride across to Tom and yell at him for scaring her, but she was unable to leave the deck chair. In fact she couldn't move at all. She just sat, her head turned to one side, staring at Tom and the sand man.

With great effort she turned her head and looked down at the sand in front of her. The tide had crept even closer – amazingly close. The water had almost reached her toes. How fast could it come in? Not that fast, surely. And was that a face in the sand? Like the sculpture – a woman's face, perfectly captured in the damp sand.

The eyes snapped open in the sand, raw and mad, and Kate woke up with a jolt in the deck chair.

'Look!' Tom said, close by. 'The water's wrecking all my sand castles!'

Kate sank back into the deckchair, sweating and shivering at the same time. She was coming down with something. That was the only explanation. She never had dreams like this. And she never fell asleep.

She stared at the patch of sand by her feet. There was no face. No eyes. Just sand worm casts and a thin, wet string of seaweed. She shivered again.

'Come on, it's time we were going,' she announced. She

stood up stiffly, her body aching from nothing. She tried not to look at the sand anymore.

'But look at my sand castles! They're total wrecks!'

'Ruins,' Kate corrected him, mustering a smile. 'Castles end up as ruins. Ships end up as wrecks.'

'It's not fair. Tomorrow will be our last day. I don't want to go home.'

She squeezed his hand and brushed sand from his damp fingers. 'Me neither. But you can have too much of a good thing.'

Tom blinked at her. 'How?'

They packed up and started trudging back along the beach towards the front. 'How can you have too much of a good thing?' Tom asked again.

'Well, you get spoiled if you have too much of a good thing. If you have too much of it you don't appreciate that it's a good thing anymore.'

'That's stupid.'

'Maybe,' agreed Kate. 'It's just a kind of saying, really.'

'It sounds like something grown-ups invented to stop kids having fun.'

'You could be right.'

'Those sand castles were my very best. I wish you could have seen them. One of them had a moat and a bridge. A *proper* bridge. I had to dig underneath with my finger.'

'Well, we can have another go tomorrow. We'll spend all day building castles if you like, the very best ones. And I promise I won't fall asleep.'

Inevitably, with the day drawing to a close, they made their way towards the sand man. He had carved the same woman in the sand again, this time with infinite artistry and care. The figure looked so lifelike that Kate felt startled.

'You've excelled yourself today,' she told the sand man.

He smiled. 'Thank you.'

'It's like she's getting more lifelike every day,' observed Tom.

'Thanks.'

'Maybe she will come alive tomorrow.'

'Maybe.'

Kate felt goosebumps. There *was* something very lifelike about the face in the sand, and she had an uncomfortable memory of her dream, where the eyes had snapped open in the sand.

'She looks... Familiar, almost,' Kate said.

'She looks a bit like you, Mum,' said Tom.

'Don't be silly.' Kate looked back at the woman in the sand. Did she look like her? No, that was stupid. The figure in the sand was beautiful and slim.

But the face... Could that be *her* face? It was hard to tell. But could that be why she felt the features were so familiar? As if she had seen them somewhere before, earlier that day? In the mirror, perhaps? Kate looked at the sand man, annoyed. 'Are you modelling her on me?'

He shrugged and smiled. 'Maybe.'

'Well don't. Come on Tom, we're going.'

'Sorry if I offended you. I didn't mean it.'

Kate forced a smile, realised that she had sounded rude. 'It's nothing. It's our last day tomorrow. Feeling a bit tense, I suppose. Got to go back to work on Monday, you know how it is...'

The man shrugged. 'Not really.'

'All this will seem unreal,' Kate continued, looking around her. 'Like a fantasy.'

'Perhaps it is.'

'Yes,' she nodded sadly. 'Perhaps.'

\* \* \* \*

The last day was bitter-sweet. Kate had to explain what that meant to Tom, and he seemed to get it. They had one last ride on the pirate boat. As they left the harbour, close in to the beach because the tide is so far out, Kate saw the sand man standing by the RNLI ramp, watching them. He raised a hand and Kate looked away, confused.

Tom didn't want to leave, and who could blame him? A beach holiday is like paradise for an eight year old. Kate had mixed feelings. She didn't want to go back to work, the humdrum life she had before, but at the same time she was tired and the seaside was starting to unnerve her. The constant cry of the gulls in the air above was starting to irritate her.

But she couldn't help hanging back at the end of the day, if only to check on the sand sculptures. Tom insisted, and Kate knew that a part of her wanted to see the sand man one last time.

They walked along the beach as people packed up to leave. The donkeys were tied together and led off the beach in a long troop, heading for the nearby fields where they lived. Men with metal detectors came out, combing the sand for coins and keys and mobile phones left by the holidaymakers. Kate and Tom watched them for a while.

'What are they doing?' Tom asked.

'Looking for metal. People drop coins and things and they get lost in the sand. Those people come along afterwards and find them with metal detectors.'

'Do they give the coins back to the people who dropped them?'

Kate smiled. 'I doubt it.'

'Why are we waiting?' Tom asked, shivering. 'I'm cold now.'

Kate sniffed, looking up as she thought she felt a spot

of rain. It *was* chilly now. Grey clouds had gathered and the sand looked dark, almost volcanic.

They walked along to see the sand man. One of the other sculptors had returned, the smiling black guy in a t-shirt that said '*Larry says hello.*' He had carved out a perfect facsimile of a lifeboat and dolphins and a rather wonderful shark. It was dynamic and exciting and truly a work of art. Many people had thrown coins onto the towel by his feet.

'I bet he gets more money than the metal detector people,' said Tom.

But Kate was looking further along the beach. There was a long stretch of empty sand, and no sign of the sand man.

She turned to the sculptor nearby. 'Where's the other one? The other sand sculptor who's been here all week.'

The man called Larry just frowned. 'Who?'

'He's young and sort of nice, with sandy hair and tan-coloured shorts. Made a beautiful woman in the sand every evening, just over there.'

Larry shrugged. 'I come here every day, love, and I don't know anyone like that.'

'But he's been here each night this week,' Kate insisted. 'I talked to him.'

'What's his name?'

'Well, I don't know.'

'He isn't here now. Sorry, but I don't have a clue who you mean. I've been coming here a long time and I don't recall anyone of that description.' The man started to pack up as the tide started to wash away at sculptures. Tom watched sadly. 'That's what happened to my castles,' he said. 'I wanted them to last forever.'

He leant against Kate as they watched the tide eat the sculptures.

'What's that?' asked Tom, pointing down into the water. 'It looks like a person.'

Startled, Kate peered at swirling sand and sea. There was the woman. A perfect sculpture, with an uncanny likeness. An icy chill ran through Kate as she recognised the face in the water. It was definitely her, virtually a reflection. But there was no sign of the sand man anywhere.

'How is she still there?' asked Tom.

'I don't know,' Kate said. 'She must have been left under the sand somehow... maybe she's just been revealed as the tide moves the top layer away. But...'

The woman's face began to melt as more water swilled around it. The eyes were removed, to reveal dark pits. The nose left a small hole as the surface of the flesh was swept away and underneath, unexpectedly, were sand-teeth. Impossibly, it was a perfect human skull made from the sand, grinning back up at Kate.

She felt a sudden horror grip her as the skull seemed to turn to look at her, to look at Tom. Kate grabbed him and pulled him close; the sand was just collapsing under the skull, surely, making it move... but then how could an arm be rising out of the surf, a bony hand reaching up, long brown fingers uncurling like claws.

'What's that?' Tom whined. 'What's happening?'

'It's just a stick,' gasped Kate. 'It's just a stick, caught up in the sand. Drift wood.'

The fingers stretched towards them, and then the arm sank back beneath the waves. Sea water foamed over it, hiding the bones completely.

For a second Kate thought she saw the sand man's face in the sand as well, smiling up at them, but then he was gone too.

gone too.

Gary McMahon is the author of a wide variety of horror novels, novellas and chapbooks, including the much celebrated *Concrete Grove* trilogy and the *Thomas Usher* books. His short fiction has been published in a variety of collections and anthologies including *Tales of the Weak and Wounded*, *The Mammoth Book of the Best New Horror* and *The Year's Best Fantasy and Horror*, as well as the portmanteau audio anthology *Thirteen*. He can be found at www.garymcmahon.com.

# SHE WHO WAITS

## GARY MCMAHON

The last time he'd stayed here, Annie was still alive.

That had been a year ago; they'd spent a dirty weekend in the little B&B on Queen's Parade, in a room that overlooked the sea. It was a wonderful time, filled with sex and wine and promises. But all that happiness ended a few months later, when Annie was taken from him.

She knew about the cancer all that time in Scarborough. She'd meant to tell him while they were here, but she couldn't bring herself to ruin the holiday. She kept it to herself for a little while longer, hoping that he wouldn't notice how tired she was, and how her hair was becoming brittle, her skin pale and ghost-like.

When she died, it was like someone had taken the

stopper out of his life and everything that was bright drained out. All that was left behind – all that remained of his relationship with his wife – was a darkness that would never shift.

He thought about this now as he looked up at the shell-like ruins of the castle. She'd loved it here. Being an entirely urban animal, Annie had adored the coast, and the sight of these castle ruins perched high up on a promontory overlooking the sea had made her face light up as if she were holding a candle under her chin.

To Ash the stones looked cold and hostile. They held no warmth or wonder: just a bunch of old stones, piled up as protection against the elements and enemies. He'd always been a pragmatist, and now he was even more so. Annie's death had hardened him more than he could ever describe.

"Beautiful, isn't it?" The old man approached him from the side. He was wearing a black raincoat and a blue baseball cap. In his right hand he clutched a walking cane with what looked like a hand-carved head – small features; a face, something cruel and uncaring.

"I'm sorry?"

"The castle," said the old man, still looking up at the ruins. "It's a sight."

"It's very...bleak." Ash pondered his choice of word, and realised that it fit.

"Aye. That'll be right. Bleak and lonely, like old bones." He grinned, glanced at Ash, and started to laugh. His face was familiar, but Ash could not imagine where they might ever have met before. It was something about the eyes, the shape of the forehead...

"Er...yeah. Whatever." Ash started to walk away, but the old man grabbed his arm, his diminutive stature belying great strength. His eyes were huge, containing a level of desperation that Ash found unsettling.

"Some nights, if you come out here and look up at the castle keep, you can see her. The one who waits." He laughed again, released his grip on Ash's forearm, and hobbled quickly away.

It was growing dark. Ash felt the urge to get away, to find some bright lights and crowds. He hadn't eaten all day. Maybe he could find a nice place where he could sit alone and watch the world go by.

As he walked towards Queen's Parade, he began to hear the sounds of traffic and the cries of revellers as they headed towards bars and restaurants near the North Bay.

The air coming in from the sea was cold, fresh and damp. It woke him up, making him feel closer to reality than he had in quite some time. He turned up a side street, away from the sea front, and found a tiny Italian place that looked quiet and comfortable, set apart from the crowds.

Inside, he sat at a table and ordered a bottle of merlot, then slowly read through the menu. It was cheap and cheerful; exactly what he was after. He ordered a seafood pasta dish from the smiling waiter and finished the bottle of red before it arrived.

"Could I have another bottle please?"

The waiter nodded. Was that a trace of judgement in his eyes, or was it pity at seeing a middle-aged man drinking alone in a popular tourist destination? Ash didn't care. He'd stopped caring a long time ago what anyone thought of him. The only opinion that mattered – had ever mattered – was that of Annie, and she was gone.

As he ate, he began to feel drunk. The restaurant started to fill up. Laughter and conversation bloomed around him like exotic flowers. He admired their beauty, but they were untouchable. He had his own flora to care for, and it had already withered on the vine.

His anger surprised him. He'd never felt bitter about being left alone, but sometimes he missed his wife so much that the longing for her company transformed into jealousy. He hated other couples for having the very thing he needed. He couldn't be happy for them; they taunted him with their closeness to each other.

A woman's laughter cut him like a knife. The sight of a kiss was like a bullet in the head. He stared at the remains of his food, his appetite waning. He cleaned the plate, but it was out of duty rather than hunger. He'd paid for this, so he would damn well finish it. Annie had never liked to see food go to waste.

There were tears in his eyes as he pushed the empty plate across the table. He drowned them with wine; alcohol helped, but never enough.

When a hen party entered the place, he raised his hand to signal the waiter. He asked for his bill, and drained the second bottle as he waited. The hen party was loud and their laughter filled the room, straining it to the point of breaking. The women wore sluttish costumes. Three or four of them were draped in inflatable plastic penises. One of them – presumably the hen – wore a partially inflated condom on her head like a hat.

He paid the bill and left the restaurant, glad of the cool air on his face as he walked out of the door.

The sound of the hen party's laughter dogged his footsteps as he made his way back down towards the North Bay, and the B&B. It was the same one he'd stayed in with Annie, a year ago. He'd booked it a week ago, knowing that it would hurt him to stay in the same place – when he'd enquired about the same room they'd used the year before, he was surprised to find it vacant. Was it a sign? Was he meant to come back here and retrace her final steps?

The landlady was in the hallway when he let himself

in. She was standing by the phone, as if she'd just finished a call. "Good evening, Mr Ash." Her smile was small, gentle. Her frame was thin. She had skinny wrists that looked as fragile as a bird's legs.

"Good evening. It's getting chilly out there tonight."

She smiled again, nodded. "Busy, too, I'll bet."

"Is the bar still open?" He took off his coat and draped it over his arm.

"The bar's always open for our guests, Mr Ash. Go ahead." She stepped to the side, indicating the door to the small lounge that served as the bar area. "I'm the same," she added. "I just can't seem to sleep without my nightcap."

The bar was decorated in a style that had gone out of date at least a couple of decades before. There were framed photographs on the wall: monochrome landscapes and street scenes, all depicting a bygone Scarborough: horse-drawn wagons, cockle-pickers in flat caps and heavy tweed coats, washer women with pale faces and dour expressions, small, shy children holding onto their dresses.

"Hello again, sir. What can I get you?" The man behind the bar was small and wide; his face was shaped like a football with features sketched upon it. What little hair he possessed was scraped sideways in an ineffectual comb-over.

"I'll have a scotch, thanks. Make it a double."

The man – Mr Mayweather, the landlady's husband – nodded and turned to the optic.

"Join me?" said Ash, on impulse.

"Why, thank you, sir. I'll have a wee tot myself, if that's okay by you."

Ash said nothing and watched the man as he poured the drinks.

"Cheers," said Mayweather, as he set down Ash's glass.

"Your good health." Ash took a swallow of the whisky. It burned his lips, the inside of his mouth, and his throat on the way down. Bliss.

"Are you enjoying your stay?" Mayweather pressed his pot belly against his side of the bar. His eyes were dull. His skin was pallid; the complexion of someone who spends too much time indoors.

"I took a walk along to the castle," said Ash. "It's quite beautiful."

"Ah, yes. I like it up there, myself. Fourth Century. Roman. An interesting structure." Mayweather took another sip from his glass. His pursed lips made it look like he was enjoying a kiss.

"I suppose it's haunted," said Ash. "I mean, most old buildings tend to have some kind of history of that kind." He smiled. He thought of the old man, the desperation in his eyes, the words he'd mumbled.

"Oh, yes," said Mayweather. "Of course. What would an ancient building be without a few ghosts?" He grinned. His teeth were bad: yellow, with a few gaps. "I suppose the best-known one would be She Who Waits."

Ash stopped smiling. He set down his glass on the bar. "Really?" he said.

The old man's words: *The one who waits...*

"Yes, this one goes back a long way. Fifteenth century, I think. A woman – the wife of a sailor or a smuggler – used to climb up into the keep to look out to sea. Her husband had gone missing. She never accepted he was dead. She kept watch for months, and then one morning they found her up there, dead from exposure. A sad story – maybe it's even a true one. Who knows, eh?"

Ash held onto his glass, but he didn't take a drink. "And her ghost haunts the keep?"

Mayweather nodded. "Yes, that's right. They call her She Who Waits. Some people have seen her up there, staring from the keep. She stands and she watches and she waits...perhaps for her long-lost lover. It's a nice story. Bullshit, but a nice little legend to talk about." He flashed his bad teeth, emptied his glass. "This one's on me," he said, and turned away to pour another couple of drinks.

That night his sleep was disturbed. He was not in his bed, in his room, he was standing beneath the castle keep, looking up. Atop the stone keep, a figure moved back and forth. He couldn't make out who it was, but he was certain that it was a woman. Was it Annie, searching for him? Was she restless because she knew he'd come back here, to be close to her?

He tried to reach out, but his hands were bound. There were no physical restraints, but he was unable to move them. His legs were mired in invisible mud. His body was heavy, like rock. He opened his mouth to call out her name, but a wind came up and snatched it away...but she knew he was there. She turned, slowly, mechanically, and raised her hands up into the night sky. Blackness writhed at her back. Her face was white and featureless. The ragged dress she wore whipped around her thin body. Cancers dropped from her armpits, scurrying away into the darkness...

When he woke up he forgot for a moment where he was. He stared into the dark, waiting for his surroundings to become clear. As the room resolved around him, he saw a motionless figure standing at the foot of the bed. Its arms were raised. Its body was indescribably thin. Then, it began to move. Like a puppet controlled by strings, it jinked sideways, arms and legs twitching, head nodding clumsily on the stalk-like neck. The figure moved around to the side of the bed, its raised arms flapping, feet dragging across the carpet. Just as it bent awkwardly towards him, about to reveal what he knew would be a blank white face, Ash woke up again, and realised that it was simply an extension of his nightmare.

He ate breakfast late, hoping that he would not be disturbed by any other guest. He wanted to suffer his hangover in peace.

Just as he was finishing his coffee, someone skulked into the room behind him and sat down heavily in a chair. Ash gulped the rest of his coffee and stood, fumbling for his coat on the back of the chair. When he turned around, there was nobody else in the room. Traces of his nightmare clung to him like promenade candy floss.

He hurried out of the B&B and breathed in the chill morning air. The sun was high; thin clouds teased the edges of the day. He headed down towards the sea, hoping that its natural beauty might help to clear his mind.

The streets were littered with chip wrappers and kebab papers. He dodged a pool of vomit as he stepped off the kerb to cross the road. It was still too early for the revellers to be up and about, but there was a fair bit of traffic on the roads.

When he reached the promenade he leaned on an iron railing at the top of a set of old stone sea steps. Coastal corrosion had been at work; the safety rail was covered with scabs of rust, the steps had been eaten away by the salt. The sand was flat and grey. The tide was out; the dirty waves lapped timidly at the beach, like a reluctant lover.

Ash turned around and looked up at the castle. From here he could see the old keep, and if he squinted against the pale sun he could make out what looked like a figure standing right at the top of the stone structure. Was it waving, or was that just an illusion? He could not tell; there probably wasn't even a figure, just a cloud, or a figment that his mind was so desperate to conjure.

He walked down to the beach, moved cautiously across the sand, and stared out to sea. A small boat inched along the horizon, dipping occasionally out of view as the sea rolled. He felt small, insignificant. The last time he'd even felt part of this world was when Annie had stood at his side, looking out at this same sea. He'd lost so much. Bits of his spirit had been scraped away. There was not enough of him left to make a dent on reality.

He walked back up to the promenade, found a small pub, and sat reading a paper that he found discarded on a stool. He drank more beer than he was used to, began to feel light-headed. Nobody spoke to him. It was as if he was becoming part of the scenery, just another facet of the fabric of the place.

He was unaware of time passing. When darkness began to fall, he paid up and left, stumbling over the step on the way out. The early evening was alive with the sound of catcalls. The revellers never gave up in their pursuit of transitory pleasures. Even out of season, they came here, trying to eliminate the humdrum aspects of their existence in an environment of sea, sand, and Happy Hours.

He knew exactly where he was going even before he started to walk in the direction of the castle. This was why he'd come here. He had been lying to himself all along. This trip was not a pilgrimage to spend time in the place where he and Annie had last been truly happy; it was a search for evidence that there was something more to life than what he could see, hear, taste...

He had come here in search of a phantom – and any phantom would do. If there was a ghost here, he would embrace it and make it his own. He would find comfort in the haunting. Because whatever ghost was here, it was better than the ones he carried around with him.

The old man was there again. He stood staring up at the keep, his face lost in shadow.

"You came back," he said. "I knew you would. We always do."

Ash turned to him, but kept his distance. He was not even sure if this man were real, or if he was simply another ghost. "What do you mean?"

"She Who Waits...she's ours. She belongs to us. She

waits for whoever wants her to wait. There's nothing complicated about a ghost. It becomes what we want it to be."

Ash wanted to say more, to ask more questions, but the old man turned away and started walking into the shadows. His legs vanished, bleeding away like a fading cinema image. The last thing to go was his head. Then, there was only the darkness, and whatever waited within it.

"I know you," said Ash, not fully understanding what he meant, or where the words had come from. They'd just felt right, like some kind of obscure truth.

When he looked up again towards the castle keep, she was there. She was always there. Always waiting.

She raised a thin arm, the ragged material of her dress hanging from it like sundered flesh, and waved at him. Her arm moved in a long, graceful arc over the top of her head. Yet still, she resembled a puppet, like the vision from his nightmare.

Ash was afraid, but his longing was much stronger than his fear, so he started to move towards the hillside and looked for a way up. A narrow path snaked up the slope, so he set off towards it, hoping that he could make it to the top. The beer he'd drunk earlier was slopping around in his stomach, making him feel unsteady. His mind was thick and heavy, like a broth.

But his feet carried him there. Again, it felt as if this had been preordained; he was meant to come here, to meet whoever was waiting.

The base of the castle keep was in darkness. It seemed as if the shadows had gathered there, forming some kind of barrier through which only he could break. He stepped over the dark threshold and entered the black doorway at the foot of the keep, and began to climb the cold stone steps that led to the top.

As he climbed, he remembered Annie's final hours. The way she'd been unable to speak, but had communicated to him by touch: the gentle weight of her hand on his arm, the pathetic grip of her weak fingers as she held his hand. Tears rolled down his face, but he was smiling. He had loved her, and he loved her still. Her death changed nothing of how he felt. He would love her for ever.

When he reached the top of the keep, the wind buffeted him and he almost lost his footing. He walked slowly across the flat stone roof, keeping his eyes fixed on the figure that stood at the far edge, looking away from him, gazing out to sea.

As he drew closer, he began to make out more details. The dress she wore was ruined; it was torn and worn thin in places, so that her bones could be seen. What little skin still covered her skeleton was clenched tight to the bone, as if she were shrink-wrapped. He could see her yellowish ribs; her pelvic girdle stuck out at an angle.

He stood behind her, wondering what he should do next. Then, while he was still pondering, she began to turn around and face him.

Her hair was like white seaweed whipping around an old rock. The side of her face was smooth, like alabaster, but as more of it came into view he saw that it was ridged and wrinkled, like tripe. The beauty he'd sensed in her began to leech away, replaced by a sort of crawling horror. She was not touching him, but he felt violated, as if a long, bony finger was searching for a way inside his body.

He realised that he'd made a mistake in climbing up here, but it was too late to turn back. All he could do was wait for her – as she had waited before him – and discover what his terror looked like.

As she turned full circle, she raised her arms. The rags hung like tattered wings. Small, twitching shapes dropped from beneath her arms and scuttled across the rooftop to tug at his legs. He felt them climbing up his trousers, but was unable to draw his gaze away from her.

The face that looked into his was featureless, but it was not a true blank. Once again, he thought of dressed tripe: pale, bloodless, ridged and creased and honeycombed, and with an unwholesomeness about it that made him gag. Her movements were clumsy; she moved in staggered bursts, like a failing clockwork toy. Darkness writhed at her back, crawling across her bony shoulders.

"No," he said. "I don't want this. I want her back... Annie. I want Annie."

A slow smile began to split the bleached-offal face, tearing it in half so that more of those small dark creatures could spill out and tumble towards him in a seething, chittering mass. He batted at his chest, his belly, but there were too many of them to brush away. They felt like cobwebs; too little substance, breaking apart at his touch. But their bite, when it came, was agonising.

These, he realised, were the pieces of his grief made solid. Much in the same way that Annie's cancer had been little more than her own rebelling, mutating cells, they were parts of his being that had turned on him, tearing him apart. He could not escape them. They were simply coming home to roost.

He fell to his knees and looked up for one final time into the torn face of She Who Waits. Still he was unclear if this were real or simply another fragment of last night's dream. Perhaps, he thought, he had never woken up after Annie died.

The gap that was the figure's face yawned wider, encompassing, and then becoming, the depth of his loss as he felt himself pulled to pieces by his grief. Annie was in there. He knew it. He had not come here in vain. All he had to do was find her, reach out a hand in the darkness and carry her home. Thinking this, he closed his eyes and let himself fall into that darkness.

* * *

The old man had waited such a long time. He had no real memory of anything, other than the ancient castle keep and the entity that dwelled there. They had both spent a long time here, waiting for the right one to come.

And here he was now; the right one. They knew the man would arrive, if they waited long enough.

He walked slowly through the early evening, almost cautious in his approach. Then, just as he was meant to do, he looked up at the remains of the castle.

"Beautiful, isn't it?" The old man approached him from the side. He was wearing a black raincoat and a blue baseball cap he'd found in a charity shop. In his right hand, he clutched a walking cane with what looked like a hand-carved head – small features; a face, something cruel and uncaring.

"I'm sorry?" said he other man – the one for which he'd waited so long.

"The castle," said the old man, still looking up at the ruins, fighting the tears. "It's a sight."

"It's very...bleak." The other man seemed to ponder his choice of word.

"Aye. That'll be right. Bleak and lonely, like old bones." The old man grinned, realised that he was about to sob with joy, and started to laugh instead.

"Er...yeah. Whatever." The other started to walk away but the old man grabbed his arm. This was it: the moment he'd been waiting for. It was time to plant the seed in this other's mind.

"Some nights, if you come out here and look up at the castle keep, you can see her. The one who waits." He laughed again, released his grip on the other man's forearm, and hobbled quickly away.

It was done. At last he was free. The moment had come full circle; history had finally repeated itself.

She Who Waits could be fed once more, and after that it was someone else's turn to set the wheels in motion. He'd taken his turn, done his allotted shift. Now his reward was due.

This time when the darkness claimed the old man, he felt like himself. He felt like Ash again. And this time his wife, his beloved Annie, was there waiting for him.

Johnny Mains is an award-winning editor, author and horror historian. Charlie Higson (Fast Show) calls him 'Minister For Horror'. He has written for SFX Magazine, Illustrators Quarterly and The Paperback Fanatic. Mains was Project editor to Pan Macmillan's 2010 re-issue of *The Pan Book of Horror Stories*. Mains is also co-editing *Dead Funny* with multi-award winning comedian Robin Ince. He has written the introduction to Stephen King's 30th Anniversary edition of *Thinner*. Mains is the author of two short story collections and editor of five horror anthologies, the latest being *Best British Horror*, out now, from Salt.

# THE GIRL ON THE SUICIDE BRIDGE

## J.A. MAINS

Elsie was woken up by the screams of her mother. Panicked, she fell out of bed, pulling the duvet with her. Her dad came into the bedroom, his face was stretched tight with grief.

"It's your brother," was all he managed to get out before he collapsed onto the floor, the bones in his body succumbing to that invisible onslaught of despair.

"Ben? What's happened to Ben?" Elsie started to scream, her voice rising to such a pitch that the empty glass on the dresser began to vibrate ever so gently.

All three sat on the sofa, silent, destroyed. The police officer was in Dad's favourite chair, a look of practised empathy on her face. Her notebook next to her, closed, on the worn arm – the place where Dad always sat his mug of tea.

"Can Elsie leave the room for a second please?" The officer wasn't surprised when the Mother grasped her daughter as if she was in danger of drowning, and held on for dear life, shaking her head; *no*.

"Very well. The person we believe to be Ben has been taken to the mortuary, and we'll need someone to formally identify him," she said softly. She glanced at Elsie who was staring at her toenails, painted a delicate blue. The young girl's face was puffy, her eyes red and raw.

Mum wailed. Dad looked lost and confused; knowing deep in his heart that he was in some way responsible for his son having hanged himself from the Valley Bridge.

*    *    *    *

It was a notorious spot, and with every death there was more pressure heaped on the council to install barriers. It wasn't just a local problem. People who wanted to end their life from all over the country had heard and had travelled to Scarborough. News of a new death was already circulating and the residents of Scarborough had reached tipping point. Ben was only seventeen and had been the first person to have hanged himself from the bridge – everyone before had thrown themselves off. At the moment he had jumped and the rope bit, snapping his neck and nearly taking his head off, a Vauxhall Nova containing a family of five returning to Galashiels in the Scottish Borders had been driving along the Valley Road.

Within the suicide note stuffed into the back pocket of his cords, Ben had written that he didn't want to be remembered like the others who had thrown themselves off – those who had severely injured innocent travellers, in one instance killing the driver of an Audi 100.

\* \* \* \*

Relatives began to visit, filling the day with more pain than the house could possibly bear, weeping aunties and uncles, sullen and confused younger cousins in tow. The phone was constantly ringing; the funeral parlour, the Housemaster of the college who promised a full investigation as to how Ben left the grounds, distant relatives.

Elsie went to her room, numbed by their aggressive

sympathy. She wanted to go into Ben's room, but was too scared to bring herself to do it; afraid of the silence and the knowledge that the room now belonged to no-one. It was his space no longer. It was just a room full of stuff.

She opened the squeaking cupboard door and pulled out her jacket and beaten up trainers. She folded the jacket and put that and her trainers under the pillow. She looked around her room, at posters on the wall, photos that were above the bed, trophies for gymnastics on top of the bookcase and then, the soft whisper of death called out to her, a seductive void that invited her to join her brother.

*　*　*　*

Elsie, at thirteen, wasn't as naive as her age may have suggested and knew the real reason behind Ben going to Scarborough College, even though they only lived in the semi-detached haven of Ryndle Walk. Ben was different, and because of that difference, was despised (?) – Elsie didn't know if that was the word she would have attributed to her Dad's feelings of her older brother – but it was close.

"Ben needs structure," was all Dad would say when she asked why Ben had been sent to college, but she had to continue to go to Scalby. The 'boys' as Mum called them (always with a slight edge to her voice) had been butting heads ever since Elsie's tenth birthday party, and it wasn't long after that that Ben was sent to the College. He would come home for the holidays, of course, and that was the time Elsie and Ben would jump on a bus and travel to Whitby, up by the Abbey, playing with holidaying children at the East Cliff hostel.

There was hardly any mention of problems at home, and if there was Ben will brush it off saying that 'Dad would come round, one day.'

*　*　*　*

Dinner was stew, brought round by the next door neighbour but one, Mrs Michaels. Dad was in his shed, drinking whisky. Mum staring into space, her face blank, rubbery.

The Reverend called round later on in the evening. Mum was a little more alert, enough to allow her hand to be patted sympathetically. Dad had stumbled upstairs and was snoring off the Grouse.

*　*　*　*

When death visits, and drapes its cloak over a particular household, all normal noises like the house groaning and settling down for the night are stilled. Nocturnal animals are nowhere to be seen, frightened by the wispy, grey aura of despair that seeps out of the very brick the house is made from.

Elsie put on her scuffed trainers and her jacket, hidden under her pillow earlier on in the day, because if she had tried to get them from the cupboard now, the noise that the door would make, a high pitched continuous screeching would wake up her parents, no matter the amount of alcohol her Dad had put away.

She opened her bedroom door very, very gently and crept out of the room, sticking to the right hand side of the stairs as she went down, the wood on the left hand side had some slight warping and would let out what Elsie thought of as a sharp cough of surprise.

Downstairs she tiptoed her way to the kitchen and to the scullery where the back door was. The key was hanging on the nail that had been hammered into the casing that ran up the side of the door. Letting herself out, she locked the door from the outside, so no opportunistic burglars would visit.

Elsie zipped her jacket all the way up to her chin and started walking, her destination the Valley Bridge.

She walked past the Ryndle Court Hotel, crossed the road and nipped through a gap in the hedge and then ran as fast as she could through Peasholm Park, through the trees, just enough light in the sky to navigate by until she was next to the artificial boating lake, staring idly at the inky blackness of the water.

Picking up the pace she walked past the cricket club, hiding behind a parked van as she spied a car coming towards her, fearing that her parents were awake and had phoned the police.

\* \* \* \*

A flap of torn police tape adorned one of the rails. Elsie walked over to it slowly, her galloping heart feeling like it was swelling up in her chest, fit to burst. She could see a solitary bunch of flowers ahead. The spot. Aware of the sea to her left, every step she took made her feel she was adrift, being engulfed by tumultuous waves on all sides. But the paving was sure underfoot, it wasn't going anywhere, the bridge wasn't going anywhere. A milk float drove past her slowly, the driver paying her no notice.

When she arrived at where the flowers were, two things sucked the air from her, threatened to collapse her there and then, have her scream so hard that she'd throw herself off the bridge to stop the agony.

Footprints on the railing. And what seemed like a deep scuff mark.

*That's where the rope was* something inside her

wailed. *He jumped! He didn't climb up and sit, then drop.*
*He jumped. He wanted his...*

Elsie bit down on her bottom lip, hard. The reality of
blood stopped her for a second.

She grabbed onto the railing and breathed in deeply,
complex organs taking in more air than she ever thought
possible. She felt *everything*. And that's when she
decided to never let go.

\*   \*   \*   \*

Elsie looked down at her digital watch; the time was
eight-thirty am. She could feel people staring at her as
they walked by. She sometimes met their gaze.

At ten o'clock, one of her school friends, Julianne
Crosby, saw Elsie and ran across. She tried to console
her, but Elsie said simply, "Don't touch me, it'll stop
everything. If you touch me, it'll stop."

"I don't understand," Julianne said, her hand hovering
above Elsie's right shoulder, fear creeping into her voice.
A part of her wanted to grab her. "What will stop?"

\*   \*   \*   \*

By eleven-thirty a small group of onlookers had surrounded her. The bridge had accepted her and Elsie accepted the bridge. From the moment her hands first grabbed the pale green railing she *was* the bridge, felt the terror, anguish, fear, confusion and freedom of every person who'd met their end here. It thrummed through her body. She felt Ben, felt his last seconds, knew his final thoughts, heard the squeak of rubber soles on metal; felt the tightening of the rope as it snapped taut...

And the bridge knew that here was someone who could take *its* pain away. Years of sadness had tainted its pale green lattice work. The paint had blistered and split to reveal blood red rust. The damage, not from the heat of the sun, but the pain of the overburdened metal which sagged a little more with each tragedy.

So the metal crept onto Elsie's skin, sank into her flesh, solidified her finger bones, her hands turning shades of mint green and rust. Elsie's breathing was calm; her heartbeat steady for the first time since she'd first heard the terrible news.

And with each breath the bridge crept a little further up her arms, delicate hairs that had been ruffled in the early morning breeze forever frozen.

All of the onlookers were local; one of them knew Elsie, knew her parents and ran as fast as he could to the nearest phone box.

*　*　*　*

By the time her parents arrived the metal had crept up to her shoulders. The Police, Ambulance and Fire Brigade were in attendance. All had frozen and were looking at her, unsure, scared even.

But as those who watched and wondered remained still, Archie Clarence, Scarborough News' Chief Reporter, arrived. He looked a little worse for wear, having been at a wedding reception in York the night before. He'd heard about Ben, someone at work had placed a phone call to him – he was the 'deathbridge' correspondent after all, but a family gathering was a family gathering. There were obligations to be met as a Clarence and so he'd stayed away. Now, he watched with the others as Elsie's Mum collapsed to the ground. Dad swore at his daughter, seemingly drunk, not seeing the way that she was, not seeing what she was *becoming*. Both were led away and Clarence took his chance to approach her. The police allowed him to, unable to think of what else to do.

"Elsie, it's Archie. You know my daughter Lillias. You've been round a few times."

Elsie turned her head a few inches. It was a laboured movement; she looked to be in considerable pain. When she talked the noise that came from her sounded metallic;

a hammer head pulling out a rusted nail from wood that will not give.

"I know you Mr. Clarence. And you'll help me?"

He didn't know how he could. The story to end all stories was there, right in front of him. He wouldn't just win prizes, accolades, notoriety. He'd have a ticket that would open any door he wished to go through. He'd be world famous. He'd be Archie *Fucking* Clarence.

He reached out instinctively, like his job taught him to console those in a bad way. His hand touched the nape of her neck and he yelped as a bolt of electricity shot through him.

And he saw *his* son.

The vision of Caleb Clarence was older than his current fourteen years and he was standing on the bridge. He was smiling. He yelled "I hate you ALL!" before jumping and cracking his skull wide open on the road a second or two later.

Elsie looked at Clarence and said quietly, "I can stop this."

And Archie Clarence understood.

He understood that if word got out, it would be the end of Scarborough, the end of their part of the world. Or worse. Caleb might not be stopped.

Something was happening that he simply couldn't

comprehend – this young girl was being eaten alive by the bridge that had seen her brother end his life.

"What do you need?" he asked.

"To be left alone. For a while."

And those were the last coherent words that Elsie uttered.

* * * *

The residents of Scarborough became Elsie's bubble. There was word put in the newspapers and broadcast on the local news that there would be major works around the Valley Bridge and that it would be a no-go area for at least a week.

No news escaped the town. All of the roads out were closed by the police. All boats were scuppered, with the bill going to a willing but scared Council which promised to pay after the embargo had passed.

Everybody in the town knew that something much bigger was going on, something important. They were happy to let it happen. They didn't know if Elsie was a sacrifice, a willing participant or if she had been struck by lightning.

At this point, all of Elsie was metal. Her eyelids blinked for the last time that morning, a slight flutter, like a dying butterfly's wings. A garbled sound, like steam being released from boiler room pipes came escaped from her.

Every inch that was flesh was flesh no more. But still she was alive, and more alive than she had ever been. She sensed the emotions of every person in Scarborough. When they were low she felt their pain. And they would come to her. She was the centre of loss and they would sit by her, this statue of grief and pay thanks to her sacrifice.

Her Dad visited each day. Talked to her, shouted at her, even took a rock to her but not a mark would be made. Elsie felt everything, not as pain, she had gone way beyond mere sensation of the flesh, but as infinite sorrow. There was no memory, just heat ebbing and flowing through her core every time he struck her.

He died of a heart attack some two weeks later.

\*   \*   \*   \*

The town slowly settled, and Elsie was regarded by visitors as a statue that happened to look out to sea. No-one remarked on her features, so intricately carved – the way that the fabric of her dress was so expertly made that it looked like it hugged those small legs.

No-one noticed the rust that utterly covered both hands but stopped at each wrist. Archie, members of the council and the Police made sure that the spot where

Elsie stood was never troubled - that the bridge was repaired as soon as a problem was reported.

The suicides stopped and Valley Bridge saw no more pain.

That's not to say that people who wanted to end their life stopped travelling there. In fact, more people than before visited the town of Scarborough, a sort of pilgrimage to their 'Suicide Sister'. They would sit with her to cry or scream or despair. Then each one would touch her. Lay hands on her. A natural instinct. An incredible calm would wash over them as they became hardwired to Elsie. They felt the undeniable love that emanated from this figure of forever and beyond. They felt the very *soul* of the bridge, and discovered the answers to every question and half question that they had. Every doubt they carried would be given a remedy. It stopped them. Elsie stopped them long enough to find strength to return home and find solace, friends and family. There would be conversation, recriminations, outbursts, tears and laughter.

But still, the suicides stopped. In Scarborough, the suicides stopped.

Elsie Tabster lives and loves for her brother.

Perhaps you've seen her.

For the last 20 years Sue Wilsea has lived on the banks of The Humber. She retired early from teaching to write, and in 2010 was selected by the Arvon Foundation as one of nine New and Gifted Writers. In 2012, Valley Press published her short story collection *Staying Afloat*; subsequently she won the Vogel short story competition, and this year *Looked After* was long-listed for the Mslexia's first novel award. Sue teaches part-time at Hull University and last year completed an MA in Creative Writing at Newcastle. She is half a *Spoken Word* performance duo with any spare time spent reacquainting herself with her husband and four children.

# SCARBOROUGH WARNING

## SUE WILSEA

It's gross the way he eats his Mr Whippy. First off he studies it like it's a Maths problem. When it starts to melt he sticks out his tongue and does a massive circular lick. Again and again he licks until there isn't a peak anymore. Then he darts his tongue in and out like a lizard and gently pushes the ice cream down into the cone. When he's nearly finished, he turns the last bit of cone upside down and sucks out the last bit of ice cream. Suppose it's like what he does to me, so you'd think it'd be sexy. It's so not.

There's other things – like the way he folds his clothes up neatly when he's undressing or how he counts out coins when he's paying for something or when he loses his rag if someone pinches his parking space. Just chill out I want to say.

Him being a bit older than me means he's obviously going to have a different outlook on life, but that's what attracted me in the first place. And anyway there's loads of things about him that are so cool, like the way he took charge when we booked in at the guest house and the cow behind the reception desk gave us a dirty look. Or the day we went out in the boat because I said I couldn't stick being inside all the time and the guy in charge, the captain or whatever, said we couldn't sit near the front even though there were seats free. So J insisted, politely mind, that if we couldn't sit where we wanted to then we'd have our money back. Course, we actually did get to be at the front even if it meant we were soaked from the spray. Not that it mattered – we had such a great laugh. You see, you wouldn't get Year 11 lads having the bottle to front up to someone in charge: they go around acting the big man but at the end of the day it's all just talk.

Scarborough's dead good. I didn't even know where it was until J showed me on Google Maps. In some ways it's just like any other seaside place with amusements and the fair and donkey rides and that. And seasides can be tacky. Mum and Dad used to take me and Sam to Southsea which was fine when we were young, but when we got old enough we realised how naff it was. Scarborough has a big sweep of a bay and then up on the hill there's the castle standing firm and tall and looking down on you like a Head teacher watching all the kids at break time. And there's some posh bits with cobbled streets. J took us for a walk into the Old Town and that was really romantic, even though I broke one of my heels. So it's not like he's bought me somewhere tacky.

The gulls get on my nerves, though. Their screeching goes right through me. Starts first thing in the morning. And they're massive! Our second night we were eating chips on the front, I dropped one and before I knew it a bloody great gull swooped down and was pecking at my feet. It had a horrible dirty yellow beak and evil black eyes, and I said I wanted to go and eat in a café or a pub, but J said we couldn't and that's when we had our first row.

'Anyway, you're too young to be in a pub.'

'What you on about? We've met up in pubs loads of times before!' We used to drive to little quiet country ones.

'It's different now.'

'So last week it was OK for me to be in a pub and this week it isn't. That's stupid.'

'No, it's sensible. Eat the rest of your chips.' J frowned and my heart turned over, but I wasn't letting him off the hook. I've always been the stubborn one. Gets me into a lot of trouble, that does.

'I'm not hungry anymore.'

'You said you were starving!'

'Well I lied then didn't I? You should know all about that!' I stood up and the rest of my chips fell to the ground.

'Keep your voice down! You're making a fool of yourself.'

'I don't care!' I shouted over my shoulder as I walked way.

But of course I did care. That was the problem. I crossed the road without looking properly and a car horn blared so I gave its driver the finger. Hoping and praying J would follow me, I went into one of the amusement arcades. The noise hurt my ears: coins falling, bells and buzzers ringing, the heavy click as the fruit machine handles were tugged down, a bingo caller, Lady Gaga's *Bad Romance* blaring out. I stood in front of a glass case near the entrance. Inside the case was a big grabber thing suspended over a mass of soft toys – rabbits, bears and teddies. You could tell they were tat: the fur trim on some of them was greyish rather than white, and on others the eyes hadn't been glued on straight. They all lay there on top of one another and it made me think of a picture we'd seen in History of the bodies in a concentration camp.

I hadn't cried then, not like some of the girls did, but I wanted to now. So I dug in my pocket, found a pound coin, and rammed it into the slot. Some crappy tune came out and shakily the grabber started to move. There was a wheel which you used to direct the grabber, but I knew it didn't make any difference so I just stood there and watched as the claws descended onto the toys and closed over nothing. Then the grabber slowly creaked its way back to the top and the music abruptly stopped.

'How fucking pointless is that!' I don't know whether I said that aloud or just in my head. It was so noisy and I was tired.

Then J's hand was on my shoulder, and he bent and kissed my neck. I got a whiff of his aftershave, my lower belly went tight and funny, and then everything was all right.

\*　\*　\*　\*

J likes discussing the past, so he tells me all about Scarborough when we're having our evening walk. I'm OK with that. Thinking about the future is scary, and as he says it's important to make the most of what we've got now. So he tells me that the town was founded around 966 AD by a Viking raider, and that in the fourteenth century Edward II gave the castle to his gay lover. Fancy giving someone a castle! That was really awesome. Then in the Middle Ages a fair started. J starts humming a song,

*'Are you going to Scarborough Fair?*
*—parsley, sage, rosemary and thyme....'*

'What's that then?'

'Don't you know it?'

'Duh! No. Obviously. Or I wouldn't be asking.'

'It's very famous.'

'Not to me it isn't.'

But I didn't get mad. I like the way he knows so much about everything. Like a Scarborough warning which is when you get no notice of an attack. Apparently the castle was once beseiged without warning.

'So when you and me fell for each other it was like a Scarborough warning?'

'Sort of. Now that there is The Grand Hotel,' He's got his arm draped over my shoulders and he squeezes my right shoulder as he points upwards 'When it was built in 1867, it had four towers to represent the seasons, 12 floors for months of the year, 52 chimneys for weeks and 365 bedrooms for the days of the year.'

'You're kidding me!'

'I'm not. It's true. And it has a blue plaque outside to mark the fact that Anne Brontë died there.'

'We're doing *Wuthering Heights* for AS next year.'

'Ann Brontë didn't write *Wuthering Heights*. That was Emily.'

'I know that!' I lied, 'I was just saying. Jesus....'

'Sorry, I didn't mean to...'

'...act like such a know-all dick?'

He laughs, 'Guilty as charged.'

'Anyway,' I continue, 'That's if I do choose English. I know I want to do Music and History but... ' I notice he is doing that frown again which darkens his face and makes me feel a bit anxious so I change the subject, 'I wish we could stay there!'

'Maybe next time.' He's curt. Sometimes the mood suddenly shifts between us like a dark cloud covering the sun, 'Time to head back.'

Things are changing. It's nearly the end of season and some of the cafes and arcades have been boarded up just in the week we've been here. It's getting darker earlier and as we walk back along the beach lights twinkle out at sea and the water scuds and hisses onto the sand. A few other people pass us but we keep our heads down and it's like we're just shadows passing other shadows.

It's not like I haven't considered the fact that J and I might be found out. I'm not some airhead who hasn't thought it all through. There's always consequences, I know that. And for a long time, in a weird and perverted kind of way, I've wanted all the secrecy to end: the lies, the covering up, the skulking about in corners. Not even my best mates know for certain, though I think they guessed something is going on. And as for Mum and Dad, just the thought of how apeshit they'll go can make me feel sick. But when it happened I wanted it to be calm, to be like when a piece of music comes to the end, and there's just that final note which rests in the moment before silence.

I never imagined the police sirens and the screech of tyres mixing with the screech of gulls, and two policemen running over the sand to grab J and frogmarch him up the slipway to the railings, and then spreading his arms wide apart and handcuffing him to the railings. Never. And they didn't need to have done all the heavy stuff because he just stands their quietly, head bowed not giving them any trouble. Not like me. I scream and curse as a policewoman puts her arms around my shoulders and tries to persuade me to go with her to the waiting police car with its crazy blue circling lights. I refuse, she says something into her mouthpiece and within minutes another car skews to a stop and two more policemen get out and make their way down the beach. Blinking away tears, I shrug off the policewoman and walk by myself towards the road, sand pulling at my feet. Once at the car I try another tactic, letting the tears run down my face and begging to be allowed to speak to J. A small knot of people has gathered to gawp and I hate them. I never imagined how grubby and used I would feel – not by him but by them.

Later, travelling back south in the custody of a social worker with bad breath and striped towelling socks, I pretend to be asleep and hear her on the phone talking about 'charges of child abduction' and 'in loco parentis', and although I know what those words mean I also know that there are no words that can hack it here, no words that can describe what J and I have. Later still I try and tell them that I will wait because I love him.

'You just thought you did,' they say, 'it was infatuation. It was what we call an inappropriate relationship.'

\* \* \* \*

I watched a clay pigeon shoot once and that's how I picture what happened to J and me: they threw our lives up into the air, took careful aim, and then shot them into little pieces. But the funny thing is I still like the seaside. We even go back to Scarborough occasionally. In the five years since that weekend very little has changed. The cliffs, sky, sea, sand: they're just the same. Loads will have happened on that beach and not just bad things like arrests, drinking, needles, hitting, punching, the guy who drowned a couple of years ago trying to rescue his dog. For most of the time there'll have been little kiddies building sandcastles and digging trenches at the water's edge, Dads playing footy with their sons, Mums minding the picnic and watching over their children. Family stuff.

J's never too keen on returning and of course I get that. But, I tell him, we don't look any different to all the other boring married couples who sit side by side on the benches, gazing out to sea as if it holds the answer to some unnamed problem. Now we can afford a decent B&B or even a hotel where we can sign ourselves in as Mr and Mrs, and not worry about what people think because the gold band on my finger is for real. There's no reason not to hold our heads up high.

Whenever I talk like that J doesn't reply but takes my hand, raises it to his lips and kisses it. I know what this means: he is contradicting me. He is saying that we are not like other couples. J was my teacher, I was under age and because of that the bastards put him on trial and then sent him to prison. And when he came out, as if he hadn't gone through enough, they put him on the Sex Offenders Register. Which I think is quite ironic seeing how little sex we have these days. As a result of being on the register he can only do casual work – cash in hand, no questions asked – and I'm on the till at Morrisons. A levels and University never happened. It would have been humiliating to stay on at school and it just showed how little everyone, especially Mum and Dad, knew me if they thought I'd give up that easily. Anyway, Sam has done the right thing. She's at Oxford now which should make up for the disappointment that is me.

I've noticed recently how J's hands have changed. Partly it's the manual work he does now. Before, when his fingers tapped on computer keys or held a pencil, they were quite soft. Now his fingerpads have hard ridges. When he touches my face the roughness grazes my skin and I have to take care not to flinch. But also the back of his hands have become a bit more translucent. If I take his hand and move it this way and that I can see the veins like thin blue snakes under the skin. Of course there are other signs that time has passed, like the creases around his eyes and mouth, but it's his hands I notice the most. When I told him this he said that mine had changed too and when I looked I saw that, as usual, he was right. When I used to play the piano every day my fingerpads were hard but now they're soft, almost pulpy. When we hold hands and our fingers entwine, it's like we have swapped skins.

I prefer going to Scarborough in winter, watching the waves pound the sea wall on North Bay, walking as near as I can and then jumping away if an especially large breaker rears over the wall and crashes down onto the walkway. I know I make J scared by doing that so if I'm feeling really mean I do it a lot and wait to see how long he can go without pulling me back onto the safety of the road. Once we visited in February and on the Saturday afternoon J said he wanted to visit the Rotunda Museum. I wasn't keen, but sometimes it's just easier to give way. At any rate, there wasn't anything else to do and it was freezing. So we paid our money and went in. Turned out it's full of geological specimens and I thought - Oh God, boring or what - so I wandered off and just drifted around playing on my phone which drives J mad. Every so often I came across J who was methodically working his way round the exhibitions, putting his glasses on and then taking them off as he alternately peered at the labels and then stood back to look at the bits of rock. Before, he would have told me all about them but not anymore. There was hardly anyone else there so it was lovely and peaceful, and gradually I stopped wandering and sat down, finding to my surprise how much I liked the place: the curvature of the walls, the absolute lack of corners. It felt like being cocooned in a time capsule. I kept thinking of all the great lumps of stone that had been hacked out from the cliffs or dug up from quarries which would have been covered in mud, moss, bugs and all kinds of shit; once in reasonably sized pieces, they would have had to be cleaned and polished before being put in the glass cases so that they could be scrutinised and admired.

There were hidden lights – blue, amber and violet - that showed the specimens off to their best, that made them gleam as if they came from different planets and had magical powers.

In the end I actually wanted to stay longer but the guy on the door came up and said it closed early in winter. He turned off the lights behind us and I gave a quick glance back. No magic. Everything looked dull and ordinary: just a collection of grey rocks sitting under dusty glass. When we came out J lingered in the doorway asking the guy how long the Rotunda had been there and so on. While we'd been inside it had started snowing and the ground was already freckled with a thin covering.

I looked at the sea which was framed by one of the arches of Valley Bridge. That's the bridge a lot of people used to jump from before they put up a high fence either side but some saddos still manage to get over. People will always find a way if they are desperate enough.


'Do you regret it?' J sometimes asks when he's feeling particularly low.

'Of course not!' I reply.


What else can I say?